HANNIBAL BARCA

THE LION OF CARTHAGE

Also by Peachill:

Red Eagle: A Native American
Inca: The Golden Sun
1453: The Last Days of Constantinople
Empress Wu: Rise

HANNIBAL BARCA THE LION OF CARTHAGE

peachill

Peachill Publishing
Chapel Hill | New York | Santa Monica
www.peachill.com

Preface

Peachill is a collaborative community of artists and regular folks who are passionate about telling authentic stories about the world we live in. We believe in a few key principles that collectively make Peachill unique:

- Creativity is an integral part of what makes us human
- Anyone can be creative
- Freelancers all over the globe are ready to make great stories together
- Regular folks want to be involved in the collaboration

We are creative animals. The act of building something new, creating something from scratch, and having a vision for the world around us is a key part of what makes us human beings. In anthropology, art is used as one of the earliest signs of civilization and it continues to be a key indicator of human progress. In neuroscience, creativity is observed as a key link to happiness and stress-relief. This is because creative pulls us out of the monotony of everyday, where our thoughts and desires are the most important thing in the universe, and gives us the perspective to be feel a part of something larger than ourselves. Part of a story, part of the human race, part of the world. This is the state of greatest satisfaction for human existence, and creativity helps us get there. It is our magic carpet ride.

Everyone is creative. In our own way, sparks of creativity fly off of each of us every day of our lives. Not everyone pays attention to these moments, and even fewer have the time to dedicate significant time to purely "creative" projects, but that doesn't stop each of us from having the ability to create. Additionally, no one is creative in a silo. Even traditional authors, whose names are printed alone on the book cover, benefit greatly from freely shared ideas. They choose the ideas that fit, discard those that don't, and change others to fit their vision. Whether every artist will admit it or not, creativity is inherently a collaborative process. At Peachill, we are transparent in our belief of artistic collaboration. You will not see a single "author" name on our cover. This book has been a team effort and could not have happened any other way. We do not see this as a radical change in creative method, but rather an honest admission of art in general.

The freelancer community around the world is large and growing. We believe freelancers are at their best when offered a structured approach to deliver the work they love. We believe excellent talent is hidden in corners that are often overlooked - young talent, international talent, career-switchers. At Peachill, all we care about is quality. We are passionate about developing talented professionals and helping them achieve their ultimate goals as artists. This process not only creates a fulfilling and mutually beneficial relationship between the platform and collaborators, but ensures a fresh flow of ideas and approaches to the work itself. We do not believe that we have the creative answer to every decision, but together we have a better shot.

Freelancers aren't the only ones who want to be involved in the creative process. What about fans? What about creative individuals who are passionate about projects but do not have the time to dedicate on a full-time basis? We do not believe that such collaborators should be left out in the cold. Peachill offers a collaborative online platform where freelancers and collaborators can trade meaningful interactions throughout the process. The platform offers the opportunity for collaborators to vote on project ideas, fund fully developed story boards, participate in key junctures of the creative process, and hear directly from the creative team as the project comes together. This collaborative approach is betting on a desire for more people to have a say in the art they are consuming, without demanding too much time. This platform will continue to evolve to create the best experience for all participants, while not sacrificing quality or transparency. We intend for all collaborators to feel real ownership in the projects in which they are involved. We intend to give credit and acknowledgement both online and within the books themselves. And we intend for collaborators to tell their friends and help us sell these books so that we can fund more books in the future.

This book is a product of that environment. We hope you enjoy it.

PROLOGUE

181 BCE, 30 miles outside of present day Istanbul

The old man hunched over a candlelit desk, his faded purple tunic clutching his shoulders. He winced as his knotty hands struggled to form each word on the vellum parchment in front of him. Sharp pain invaded the knuckles of his right hand, battling with his willpower to continue. He lifted his sleeve from the page to avoid smearing the ink.

A sliver of sunlight squeezed through a crack in one of the boarded up windows. Dust motes floated in the stale air.

The man's eyes strayed to the candle's flame. The wick burned still and hot over what remained of the wax stub. Melted wax pooled in the brass candleholder, waiting to drown the flame. How was it that the wax that kept a candle burning could also bring destruction to the flame? Was it irony or betrayal?

A memory assaulted him. Shouts. Screams. The smell of dirt and blood. The hard pounding of adrenaline in his temples as he feinted left and swung right, slashing through the thin necks of one enemy after another, spilling blood and severing heads with each calculated movement. They had chased strong at the heels of victory, but had tired. The country was weary of the fight. They blamed their general for bringing the war to their doorstep, to their whitewashed walls and sandstone hills.

Carthage has died without you.

Those words had replayed themselves in his mind every day since the day they'd been spoken, tearing at the bitter hole in his heart. For all his fighting, all his wounds and sacrifices on his country's behalf, it was the enemy who spared his life. How could his fiercest rival have more honor than his own countrymen? He clenched his thigh muscle, feeling the twinge there that had grown worse with age.

The twinge pulled him back to the present, and a sense of urgency dulled his pain. The story of the great city of Carthage—the pearl of the Mediterranean—would be heard. Carthage had once brought light to men's eyes, riches to their families, and lust to the hearts of her enemies. All of Africa aspired to her beauty and greatness. All of the known world sought her wealth and power.

He sat up a little straighter. His spine tingled from his hunched posture and he pressed a fist into the small of his back to stretch it.

He would finish this manuscript. It was the only way the world would ever know of Carthage. And perhaps one day Carthage would remember herself.

The old soldier returned to his careful script.

CHAPTER 1

241 BCE, Battlefield Outside of Carthage

Carthage, the prize of the Sahara, was blanketed by a smoky haze. The watchtowers that still stood gazed through the cloud and over the smoldering bones of the fallen city. The skeletons of the shops, baths, amphitheater, temples, and villas gasped their final smoky breaths, and the streets lay desolate, teeming only with blood and the last hungry wisps of fire.

The carnage of the city pointed north to a great battlefield, where the city's purple-clad protectors had fallen. Only a few were alive enough to crawl away, struggling on shaky arms and legs past the bodies of their comrades and enemies alike.

Spears stood on end, buried in skulls and hearts. A legionnaire's head rested several feet from his corpse. Another man gasped under the weight of his dead horse, moments from death. Whether clad in Carthaginian purple or Roman red, they had met the same end. Every breath of wind seemed to carry another plea to Eshmun or Apollo, another soldier's final breath. A moan leaked into the air and floated away.

A boy walked methodically through the battlefield, weaving his way through the armored mayhem surrounding him.

His younger brother followed a few paces behind him.

A lion fed on a corpse nearby, unnoticed by the boys.

"Close their eyes," the boy said. "Take any metal you can carry." He lifted the bronze armor from the dead man at his feet, pulling until the body rolled over and gave up its breast-plate. He stumbled under the weight of the heavy armor, but he didn't drop it. He was stocky and strong. He placed the armor over his own shoulders and straightened the breastplate.

His eyes carried an expression of grim determination as he folded the purple-cloaked soldier's arms over his chest and closed the eyelids. He worked with keen focus, surveying his surroundings with every movement he made.

His brother pulled a knife from a fallen soldier's belt with thin, shaking hands. His handsome features wore a mask of bravery, but his eyes flickered with fear as he looked down on a pale-skinned Roman whose face had frozen mid-contortion.

Spying the younger brother, the lion began to creep near. When the boy finally looked up, panic flashed across his face.

The lion crouched low to lunge at him.

"Hannibal!" the boy shouted for help, closing his eyes.

The lion sprang forward.

Hannibal took a breath and shoved his brother out of the lion's path.

The lion's front paws snagged the boy's tunic, toppling him to the ground and tearing the tunic. With teeth and claws bared, the lion lunged again for the smaller boy.

Hannibal grabbed a dagger from a nearby soldier's belt. Acting quickly, he ran at the lion, knife first, piercing its side. The lion roared and spun to face him.

"Get away!" Hannibal yelled to his brother.

His brother scampered across the ground on all fours and cowered behind a dead man's shield.

Hannibal backed up two paces, knife at the ready. His mouth was dry and his pulse thundered, but his mind was calm. He couldn't overpower or outrun the beast, but he could outsmart it. He took another step back, knocking his heels against the soldier whose armor he wore.

The lion sprang again.

Hannibal threw himself over the corpse's chest in a backward somersault. As he returned to his feet, the lion's great jaws snapped onto the side of his face.

Acting on instinct, Hannibal swung the dagger into the predator's face. The thing growled and bit harder.

This is not how I die, he thought. *I refuse.* Adrenaline surged through him, and he slashed at the lion's throat, striking a jaw muscle. The lion's hold on him went slack for a split second.

He somersaulted again, out of the lion's jaws, realizing that he'd dropped his dagger. He reached blindly for another weapon as blood poured down the side of his face.

The furious animal gnashed its teeth, plunging forward again with blood dripping from its eyes and neck.

Hannibal's fist closed around the cold hilt of a sword. He lifted it up and saw that it wasn't a sword at all, but a corpse's arm, stiff with rigor mortis. The lion's hot breath fanned his face as it landed on top of him, and he did the only thing he could do: he used the arm to block the lion's jaws, thankful that the crunch of bone was not his own. The arm tore from the body.

Hannibal grabbed a shield from the dirt, and with the force of desperation, he swung the shield at the animal's face.

The lion fell back a pace, stunned.

The glint of a sword in the dirt renewed Hannibal's vigor. He grabbed it and spun, anchoring his left heel in the dirt and using his own body mass to propel his sword hand around with greater momentum. The whole world slowed until time seemed like nothing more than the slow linkage of individual milliseconds. The sword appeared to float on a wave of air, angling slightly upward and then slicing the lion's fur, skin, and meat, piercing its trachea and then its esophagus where the jawbone meets the tender skin under the ear.

The beast made one final attempt to lunge.

Hannibal felt himself falling, and he twisted his body to face the lion, pulling the sword around one last time to point at the animal's lungs.

The animal's weight pushed the sword from Hannibal's hand, shoving the hilt into his hip where the armor didn't protect him. He scrambled from the path of the collapsing lion, scooting backward on his hands and rear.

The lion didn't move.

Hannibal's breath came in painful gasps. He looked around for his brother, who crept from behind the shield.

"Your eye," his brother said, pointing to the blood that poured down the side of Hannibal's face.

"Be more careful, Hasdrubal." He looked pointedly at the lion's body. "This body could have been yours." He stood on legs that shook as adrenaline drained from his body. He picked up the bloody dagger from the dirt and threw it at Hasdrubal's feet. It stuck tip first in the ground.

Hannibal put a hand to his eye and wiped at the blood that streamed from his face and neck. The injury began to throb.

"Do not wipe the blood away," a deep voice said from behind them. "It's a badge of honor."

Hannibal and Hasdrubal turned to face their father, the great General Hamilcar Barca, who sat straight and proud on a blood-spattered horse. His eyes were hard and resolute, but his face and body gave away his fatigue. He had saved Carthage on this battlefield, but he had lost a long, decimating war against Rome in the process. The Carthaginian navy was plundered and sunk. Territory was lost. Thousands were dead.

The General looked Hannibal in the eye, waiting.

"Yes, father," Hannibal said. He knew without asking that Carthage's final battle had cost a lot. He had merely to look around him to see that. But he was relieved to note the battle had not taken his father's pride. With pride, there may yet be hope.

"Remember who your enemy is today, boys, as it will be so for all of your days," the battle-hardened general said. The lines of his face sank more deeply, aging him before their eyes.

"Rome is my enemy," the brothers said at the same time. The words settled into Hannibal's marrow. He drew himself straighter and looked his father in the eye.

His father looked at him for a long, hard moment before flicking his eyes at Hasdrubal. "Come. The war is over. Much is to be done." General Hamilcar turned his horse away and wove through the bodies toward what was left of the great city.

His two sons followed behind him.

Peace would now reign in Carthage, but only because neither the Romans nor the Carthaginians had any soldiers left to die.

At least for now.

CHAPTER 2

231 BCE, Carthage

Not even the ravage of war could keep Carthage down. Under the blessing of Baal and Astarte, she grew from ashes to splendor once again. In the brightness of day, the sandstone hills around her glimmered pale yellow. Her walls and spires, clothed in white plaster, lit up like marble and glinted like magnesium. Her golden gates, which illuminated all around them, could have guarded heaven itself. As the sun fell down to worship her at the close of day, her walls and windows glowed like fiery opal. Her very existence was praiseworthy of the gods, and the gods, in turn, filled her cobbled streets and square stone turrets with a mystical swell of power and truth that captivated all who looked on her.

At the mouth of the agora, a fountain carved in the likenesses of Baal-Hammon and Tanit stood. Water flowed happily from the mouths of the statues in a show of blessing and vitality. Temples to Baal, Astarte, Melgart, Eshmoun, and Shalim lined the agora. The salty smell of roasting sacrifices and incense wove between the temples and filled the agora. They wafted through the streets to the marketplace, where they mingled with mint, cinnamon, saffron, caraway, and olive oil. Orange blossoms dripped from rooftop gardens and shop windows, catching on a slight breeze and swaying like young priestesses dancing before the gods.

This morning they seemed to dance with greater anticipation. Traders from Libya and Numidia cried out across the public squares, advertising handcrafted obsidian baubles, carved ceramics, jewels, and exotically patterned cloths, but even they had to work hard to be heard over the hum of excitement lacing the air.

"Are you going to the fight?" a young man asked a stooped old vendor selling a cart of figs. He handed over a coin.

"I expect so," the old man said. "Should be interesting to see if young Barca is anything like his father. Rome might finally get what's coming to her."

"My money's on the Hanna boy. He's bigger. Older. Plus it's time the Hannas had their due. Diplomacy before war, I say."

The old man handed over a bag of olives. "You're too young to remember the war. If Rome wants war, Rome will have war." He spat out Rome's name as if it tasted bad on his tongue. "I only hope young Barca shows himself to be a worthy opponent. There'll be no Hannas offering to lead an army into battle."

The young man laughed good-naturedly and disappeared between stalls.

Beyond the markets, servants and housewives in stout stone houses hung out the linens to dry. Their fingers fumbled with eagerness. A cobbler across the street stepped out of his shop and shut the door behind him. Children shrieked and shoved each other as they scampered in the direction of the amphitheater on the north side of the city. Men and women alike set a brisk, excited pace.

The amphitheater sat tall and proud and noisy with the hot breath of ten thousand people thirsty for a fight.

Today would see Carthage's two most powerful clans competing for their honor. The Barcas had long ruled Carthage, defending her borders from those who lusted after her riches, founding cities up and down the Iberian peninsula, and opening new trade opportunities with the surrounding territories. It was Hamilcar Barca who had brought the cornucopia of Spain's bounty to Carthage's doorstep. Under his leadership, Carthage had been preserved and restored to the thriving jewel of history. His proponents believed that without him, Carthage would have been forever lost to Rome. Today, his son, Hannibal, was fighting against Ida Hanna to uphold the family honor, to prove that he was worthy to continue in his father's footsteps.

The Barcas' rivalry with the Hanna clan was as old as the city herself. Whoever held the edge controlled the city, not only during peace, but especially at war, and for many years. The Hannas had always been on the brink of finally snatching that power for themselves. Many in the city hoped they would. It hadn't been long enough for them to forget the crippling losses that Rome had inflicted on them under Hamilcar Barca's leadership ten short years ago. Perhaps the Hanna clan's more natural bent toward politics would at last win the day.

But today's match wasn't a political debate; it was a contest of strength. It was a tradition as old as the clans. Every time the new heirs of the two clans came of age, a public wrestling match determined which clan would continue to carry the power.

With each passing second, the stadium became louder and more packed, and the betting pools became more fervent.

The golden sand of the wrestling floor was smooth and hot. While the cumulative murmurs of thousands of voices thundered across the expanse of the stadium, not a whisper of wind had yet disturbed the sand.

General Hamilcar and his son stood at the edge of the sandy floor. Hannibal's nerves didn't appear in the set of his face or his stance. His sense of control well exceeded his eighteen years. The upraised scar across his right eye made him fierce; he was a boy who had already fought for life and won.

His father frowned. He was a solid man of stern countenance. He had led the Carthaginian forces on countless military campaigns abroad and at home, been both the victor and the defeated, and had survived all of it. The only sign of his nervousness was in the line that creased the space between his dark eyebrows.

"You are a Barca, a lion of Carthage," the General said in a gravelly voice.

Hannibal met his father's eyes unflinchingly. "Yes, Father." He held still except for his eyes, which darted around the arena every few seconds as though he expected an ambush at any moment. He could see Ida's father standing across the arena, thin, menacing, and glaring at him as if he was, indeed, thinking about a pre-wrestling match ambush.

"Prove yourself to your city."

Hannibal gave a quick nod, looking into his father's eyes. From his periphery, he saw Ida Hanna step away from his father on the other side of the arena and make his way to the middle.

Hannibal jogged to meet him, refusing to appear reluctant.

The crowd quieted and Hannibal blocked out everything nonessential. He studied his opponent. Ida was taller, thinner, and a few years older than him. His hawk eyes shot spears at Hannibal, and the corner of his mouth turned up at one corner in a sneer. Ida had always been quick to act on his emotions, Hannibal knew. It was a trait that would do Carthage little good in the face of battle.

Hannibal, on the other hand, was methodical, calculating, and had always controlled his emotions with an iron will. He looked his opponent in the eye coldly, giving none of his feelings away. They stared each other down for a sizzling moment. Hannibal waited.

Ida moved his foot first.

Hannibal's face didn't change, but inwardly he grinned; Ida was too impatient.

As they circled each other, the crowd erupted in screams and jeers, reminding him that this wasn't a children's game but a battle for the future of Carthage and his family.

Hannibal narrowed his focus and the raucous fell away. He banished everything from his mind – the searing sun on his skin, the icy glare from Ida's father, the smell of sweat and dust – until he was conscious only of his beating heart and the smirking foe in front of him.

He lunged at Ida, putting all of his strength into a blow to Ida's midsection.

Ida absorbed the charge with a step back. He laughed,

ending his peal of laughter with a snort.

Rage trickled through Hannibal's veins and fueled his resolve. Ida had always lorded his superior age and height over Hannibal, and Hannibal had always let him say what he liked. Today that ended. He lunged once again, this time clenching his arms around Ida's waist and pushing him back a few more steps.

Hannibal held tightly to Ida and pushed a little harder. He carefully controlled his breathing. If he could control his breathing, he could control himself.

"Is this all you've got, little Barca?" Ida said. He dropped his elbow across the left side of Hannibal's chin and shoved his other fist into Hannibal's gut.

Hannibal felt the breath leave him, but he held his grip around Ida's waist. He felt blood sliding from his nose and watched it drip to the ground under him. He looked up, catching his father's eye.

The General nodded once at him.

Hannibal inhaled quickly. He dropped his foot back, swung his hip for leverage, and thrust Ida into the air and over his head. He twisted his arm, and Ida flipped over and sprawled facedown in the sand.

"Do you yield?" Hannibal said.

Ida didn't respond. He pushed himself to his knees, spitting dirt at Hannibal's feet.

Hannibal was faster. He grabbed Ida's neck in the crook of his elbow, flipped him to his back, and threw him to the ground again.

Ida grunted.

Hannibal pressed his knees into Ida's stomach, held his

shoulders down with his arms, and rammed his head into the front of Ida's skull, sinking it deeper into the sand and causing dust to billow around his head. Drops of blood and sweat fell from Hannibal's face to Ida's and disappeared into the red river that flowed from Ida's nose.

Ida coughed and gasped, struggling for air. He tried to grab Hannibal's leg and throw him off, but Hannibal rammed his head into Ida's face once more.

"Do you yield?" Hannibal barked.

Ida sprayed blood into Hannibal's eyes.

Hannibal stared down at him, refusing to blink.

"Yield!" Ida said.

Hannibal tamped down the elation that flooded through him and leaned into Ida. "Hannas are politicians," he said. "Leave the fighting to the men."

He removed his knees from his opponent's stomach and stood.

The deafening roar of the crowd filled the stadium. He looked around him. This was a sport to most of them, he thought. To him, it was life. Without a bow or wave, he jogged back to his father, and the two left the stadium without ceremony.

Alone in the tunnel with their victorious thoughts, General Hamilcar leaned toward Hannibal and said, "Our ancestors have built this city brick by brick. While the Barcas control Carthage, no harm will ever come to her."

With his ferocious scar covering one eye and blood smeared and dripping from the rest of his face, Hannibal was now a warrior.

"Yes, Father," he replied.

CHAPTER 3

228 BCE, Barca Family Altar, Carthage

Though the Barca clan led the city and its people, their compound didn't betray any sense of superiority. A rectangular, two-story structure with whitewashed walls, it could not have been plainer. The Barcas were proudly utilitarian.

Deep inside the compound, a windowless room housed the family's altar to Baal, the foremost god of Carthage. Smelling of old blood and incense, its untreated bricks glowed gray in the eerie candlelight.

Hannibal stood before the altar. He wore bronze armor that glinted in the dim light with his every movement. Though he hadn't grown in height, his shoulders were broader, and the muscles of his forearms cut deep grooves as he picked up a knife hanging next to the altar and unsheathed it.

A young goat hung over the altar before him. The upraised scar over his right eye lent a shadowed ferocity to his gaze as he sliced through the goat's throat. He watched its blood spatter down the sides of the altar until it calmed to a steady drip. Then, he knelt in prayer.

"I ask for the strength of Baal in my ultimate pursuit. Grant your wishes upon me that Carthage will always triumph over her foes, above all, Rome," he prayed. He placed a symbol of Rome, a wooden figurine of a soldier wearing a painted red tunic, upon the altar. The goat's blood dripped on top of the figurine. A drop of blood slid down the figure's face and torso, landing at its feet.

Another drop fell on the figure, rocking it infinitesimally, but it remained standing.

Hannibal waited several long moments for Baal to speak. He heard only the drips of the goat's blood on the cold stone altar. A feeling of apprehension trickled through his body. He resisted the urge to shiver. He was to accompany his father to meet the Oretani King at the Ebro River. The King of the Oretani nation was the last resisting Iberian king left for General Hamilcar to conquer. The king had requested a meeting with the General, a visit that could permanently unite Spain and Africa against Rome.

Hannibal didn't feel nearly as confident as his father. After all, the pass to the Ebro was narrow, secluded, and several weeks journey away. The scouts had reported that the jagged cliffs along the road would make any escape difficult once they entered the narrow gorge along the river. Why had the King requested that meeting place in particular? It could be a trap.

"I will consult the sky as your oracle," Hannibal said, resuming his prayer. "The stars are the only true written words of the gods."

After a silent moment, he rose from the floor and left the room.

CHAPTER 4

Barca Great Hall, Carthage

Lady Barca stood inside her balcony on the east side overlooking the great hall at the front of the compound. Something felt wrong, but she wasn't sure what. The gray and red tiles that methodically checkered the walls along the ceiling glowed in the sunlight, as usual. She personally saw to their cleaning every week. Square, undecorated pillars lined the front hall on two sides, holding up the balcony she stood on as well as a balcony directly across from her. On the north end of the hall sat a wooden chest that held the Barca family's collection of maps. In front of the chest was a plain, stout table that was used for conferring over battle plans. On a rare occurrence, it was used for leisure. Right now, it stood empty.

Today was not a battle day; it was just a friendly meeting. So why couldn't she shake the feeling that something was amiss?

Concealing herself behind her bedroom curtain, Lady Barca watched as her husband, General Hamilcar, entered the hall below her. An attendant approached, handing him a sword. He strapped it to the belt at his side.

"Hannibal," the General called, his voice ricocheting

against the stone walls like quiet thunder.

Lady Barca had always loved the sound of his voice. She allowed herself a small, private smile.

The echo died.

No response.

Her younger son, Hasdrubal, rushed into the hall below. He was dressed in full armor and moved awkwardly in it. He looked more fit to rule from a throne than a cavalry mount. In that moment, his pretty face lit with eagerness and his long, lean fingers rested on the hilt of his sheathed sword. His optimism didn't belong in battle.

Lady Barca pressed her lips together. It seemed like just yesterday he was clinging to her skirt.

"Father, I'm ready," he said.

General Hamilcar ignored his younger son. "Hannibal! Now!"

"Father," Hasdrubal said once again, his voice rising in pitch as he tried to get the General's attention.

General Hamilcar still didn't look at him. "As discussed, you will stand guard at the House of Barca. Your mother and sister depend on your sword. If we should fall, Carthage will depend on your strength."

Hasdrubal's eyebrows drew together in a scowl.

Lady Barca's heart went out to Hasdrubal, even while she understood the wisdom of her husband's decision. Hasdrubal was handsome and charming, but he had neither the cunning intelligence of his older brother nor the daring bravery of his father.

Hannibal finally emerged in full armor. His purple tunic showed beneath the bronze armor as he strode resolutely toward the front door, meeting his father's eyes.

While Hasdrubal bounced slightly on the balls of his feet, Hannibal stood before the General without moving. He had campaigned with his father in Iberia for several years and had seen enough to have lost the blissful excitement of a boy going on his first mission. Pride, perhaps. Dignity, to be sure—but no excitement.

"It's time," the General Hamilcar said.

Lady Barca watched her older son's face. She saw the smallest flicker of unease cross his eyes as he glanced in her direction, but the set of his jaw showed only determination. She wanted to believe that she had imagined the expression, but instead, her own apprehension grew.

Hasdrubal stepped forward, boldly putting his hand on his father's arm to stop him. "I request permission to join you on the—"

General Hamilcar whipped around, leading with his right fist. It connected with the bridge of Hasdrubal's nose, swiftly snapping it and causing a river of blood to issue forth.

Lady Barca didn't wince. To be a Barca was to fight.

Hasdrubal staggered back and dropped to his knees. Other than a blink of pain, his face was carefully stoic. He rose, letting the blood drip freely down his face onto his pristine breastplate.

"A soldier takes orders," General Hamilcar said.

Lady Barca shifted her weight as her sixteen-year-old daughter joined her at the window. Lady Barca felt Sapanibal's questioning eyes on her but kept her gaze riveted to the scene below.

"It doesn't seem fair that Father always favors Hannibal,"

Sapanibal whispered.

"Is that what Hasdrubal told you?" Lady Barca said. "Tell me, then, if all of Carthage were at stake, would you choose Hasdrubal as your champion?"

Sapanibal said nothing. Lady Barca bit back a sigh. Her daughter was beautiful and innocent and far too happy to think about something so distant as war. She had been barely more than a baby at the end of the last war. She had only known peace. *May it always be so*, Lady Barca thought, but her intuition told her that change was imminent.

Hasdrubal looked up to her in the balcony. Lady Barca looked back at him, guarding her expression.

His neck dipped ever so slightly.

Hannibal gripped his brother's arm in the two-handed Carthaginian handshake. "Don't be eager. Your armor will not rust." Hannibal's back was straight, but he stood without a trace of superiority.

Lady Barca studied the struggle in Hasdrubal's face. Resentment and anger battled with wounded pride and brotherly love. The two brothers exchanged a long look before Hannibal joined his father.

Hamilcar looked up at her at last as he turned to leave the compound. Then he was gone.

CHAPTER 5

Outside Carthage

The Barcas, surrounded by the Sacred Band of soldiers sworn to protect Carthage's greatest general, crested a hill outside of the city. Their black armor shone over their purple tunics and their dark faces showed nothing but grim loyalty. Many of them had followed General Hamilcar as he conquered cities throughout the Iberian Peninsula. Others helped him defeat Rome all those years ago.

Hannibal looked to his right. The sea glowed turquoise near the shore and violet in the depths, seeming to radiate Carthage's energy and beauty. He turned in his saddle for a final glimpse of the city before descending the hill. Light reflected off of her walls and towers, a resounding praise to the gods for bringing back her glory. Love swelled in Hannibal's chest. Carthage had overcome so much evil, and he would fight to his last breath to keep Rome from tearing her down again.

A band of whooper swans honked nearby.

He faced forward in his saddle. Clumps of esparto grass swayed in the slight breeze, nodding fluffy yellow heads at the passing band. Gum trees rose up around them on spindly trunks, pushing green, leafy tufts toward the cloudless blue sky. A group of gazelles grazed peacefully for a moment. Then one looked up suddenly, and all of them bounded away in great soaring leaps. They looked so graceful and free, but they lived from one moment to the next at the mercy of surrounding predators. Hannibal wondered if there was a lion nearby, but it was just as likely that the gazelles fled from the band of soldiers passing by on the road. The Sacred Band was every bit as lethal as a lion. The swords strapped at their sides could be in their hands in a blink, and his father's the fastest of all. They were the lions of Carthage. Hannibal smiled. His scar wrinkled around his eye, reminding him that, in fact, he was stronger than a lion, and had been since he was a boy.

For minutes, hours, days, he heard only the snaps of the brush under the horses' feet, an occasional animal snort, and the minimum of conversation required to set up camp for the night and pack it up in the morning. After boats carried them from the arid African terrain to the Iberian Peninsula, the ground became damper and the plants turned greener. Still, the summer sun beat on them from above.

Hannibal looked up at the sky, wishing it was dark so he could see the stars and know what the gods knew. What did this meeting with the Oretani hold for them? As they journeyed, the nights had clouded over. The gods were silent. Old cork trees with their gouged sides and gnarled arms twisted in desperation. Were they a sign from the gods? A warning? Hannibal forced the idea from his mind. The mission was simple, he reminded himself. His father knew the risk, and he was confident enough to take it. The men they'd sent ahead to scout the valley had found no threats waiting there.

The horses trudged on until the road began to sink into the entrance to the Ebro River gorge.

The General pulled his horse to a stop and the men stopped around him. The General looked at Hannibal expectantly. It was a quiz, of sorts, though everything had already been decided.

"The scouts have cleared the road," Hannibal said. "We have safe passage to the meeting location." It had been true a few short hours ago. He hoped it remained as true now.

"What do you make of this request?" the General asked. "The Oretani have long supported Rome. Why would they switch allegiance now in peacetime?"

Another quiz. "It may be a ruse," Hannibal said, but then followed it up by saying, "but it's worth our time. If we can unite all of Iberia, Rome will not threaten our shores again."

The General nodded brusquely and looked around solemnly at each of his men. Eliminating Rome's perpetual threat was the most important mission they could accomplish. He spurred his horse forward.

As they descended into the gorge and followed its path along the river, Hannibal's eyes trailed along the jagged cliff tops above them for signs of trouble. The thunder of the river current echoed off the rock faces on either side of it. Was the river as violent as it sounded? He glanced down at the water. It moved quickly, but not rapidly. He looked across to the other side, scanning its width. It shouldn't take them long to cross it. Minutes, perhaps.

When the General gave the word, the Sacred Band spread out along the crossing. They hesitated only a fraction before they ran their horses neck deep into the surging water. Froth pressed along the horses' bodies as they pushed further into the river.

General Hamilcar looked over at Hannibal. "Ready to get your boots wet?" he asked. Not waiting for Hannibal's response, he plunged into the river, and Hannibal followed closely behind him.

The cold water pulled at his armor as they struggled to the middle of the river. Every step forward his horse took was a fight to maintain balance. Even staying atop his horse took concentration, as the current swept at his legs, crawled into the armor that protected his shins, and tried to steal them both.

It hadn't looked this strong from the bank, Hannibal thought. His apprehension grew. They had made it this far, but if the Oretani were planning an ambush, now would be the perfect time. He glanced around him, flicking his eyes up the sheer rock walls that lined the river and down to the brush and trees that stooped over the shore.

His vision was drawn to a silvery glitter hidden in the tree line that the Sacred Band was slowly approaching. He squinted and saw an arrow pulled taut along a bowstring under the shade of the vegetation.

Adrenaline shot through him. His hands tightened on his horse's mane.

"Ambush!" he shouted. "Protect the General!"

He dismounted and struggled to reach for the reins of his father's horse. The Sacred Band tried to draw their mounts closer, but they were too spread out. The current slowed their progress, threatening to pull them off course and downstream.

Arrows spiked through the air from the opposite shore, pounding the group mid-river. One guard was hit, and then another, as they fell from their struggling horses. The river pulled them flailing downstream and out of the range of the arrows.

Hannibal pushed harder against the current, finally grasping the General's reins. His muscles burned from the effort of staying upright.

"Get back on your horse," General Hamilcar said to him. His face was dark and illegible. "The river will suck you down."

He searched frantically for an idea that might save them, but his sword was useless against flying arrows.

His horse struggled a couple of arm lengths away from the General's, and he turned to follow the General's orders. As he reached for his horse's back, an arrow pierced Hannibal's back. The reins flew from his hand as he stumbled, and the water pushed him a few paces downstream. He struggled to pull himself upright. He didn't feel the pain, only the thunder of blood hammering in his ears. This was his fault. He had kept silent about his misgivings.

His father had known the risk, he reminded himself, stomping down the thought. He found tenuous footing and shoved against the current toward his father, putting the energy of his growing panic into muscling forward.

From the opposing shore, the Oretani rushed into the river to their ankles, bows drawn with fresh arrows. Their faces were unforgiving as they loosed their strings.

Hannibal ducked an arrow aimed at his head and tried to count them. They outnumbered the remaining force of the Sacred Band easily. They refreshed their bows, and more arrows flew at General Hamilcar all at once. He raised his shield, and the arrows hit the shield and fell into the water.

"Father!" Hannibal shouted. He surged against the current, making only marginal progress. Helpless fury threatened to overwhelm him. *Your fault, your fault, your fault*, the echoing river said.

He inched closer, thinking through the motions he would have to take to pull his sword on the attackers. *Get closer. Closer. Closer.* His progress was too slow.

More arrows flew at the General, and again he raised his shield. The General urged his horse forward enough to raise himself out of the water a few inches. He drew his sword and glared, daring the Oretani to come closer. A few took the dare, and the second they were close enough, General Hamilcar kicked his horse forward, and, in a swift slicing motion, knocked their heads from their bodies.

War cries rang out along the bank. A Sacred Band soldier leaped to the General's side in time to take a deathly arrow to the heart. The General twisted the shield rapidly.

Hannibal reached his father's side a second after an arrow slid through the General's left shoulder blade from above. Hannibal looked up and saw the enemy peering over them from atop the cliff.

"Father!" he shouted.

His father turned and their eyes locked as they both struggled, Hannibal struggling for each step and Hamilcar for his next breath.

"Lions of Carthage, boy!" the General shouted over the roar of the Ebro. With his shield, he knocked Hannibal's head, throwing him off balance for the final time.

Stars speckled his vision. He struggled against the blackness engulfing him. As he drifted farther and farther away, he strained for a glimpse of his father. The General stood alone, fighting to his death, his men slain or washed downstream. His horse stumbled and fell beneath him. With rabid desperation, the General cut down one Oretani soldier after another, shouting until the weight of his injuries pulled him under the water for good.

At last, Hannibal lost consciousness.

He washed ashore a few hours later with the survivors left of the Sacred Band. He remembered nothing of the journey home except for the look on his mother's face when she saw him through the compound gate. He didn't have to say anything; she knew at first glance.

CHAPTER 6

219 BCE, Barca Compound, Carthage

Nine years later, the morning sun streaked through the slats in the balcony and fell across the bed where Hannibal slept next to his wife. Sophonisba was a Numidian beauty with smooth, ebony skin. Her eyelashes rested on her cheeks like silky black veils. Her features were angelic and peaceful in her slumber, though the arch of her brow suggested strength and that she was a woman not to be trifled with.

Her eyes opened, and she curled into her husband, pressing the small of her perfectly curved back into his stomach. Their marriage began as a political alliance. She was the daughter of a Numidian nobleman, and the Barcas of Carthage needed good relations with Numidia in case Rome took Africa to war again.

Sophonisba watched the violet curtains that danced in the window and drew her gaze to the breathtaking view of Carthage beyond the balcony. The city glinted pink and white in the bright morning sun, wrapped in the turquoise Mediterranean bay that was so clear she could make out shadows of the coral and seaweed underneath it. Across the bay, morning fog retreated up the hills, glowing with a haunting blue in the morning light.

The political well-being of their countries had pushed them together, but they had since fallen in love. Rumor had it that the Romans believed love in marriage was vulgar. She smiled. All the more reason to indulge it.

The early morning heat stirred her spirit and awakened her desires.

"I know you're not asleep," she whispered into the hot air.

Her husband stirred. "I thought I was before you mentioned it."

"You never sleep when the sun is out," she said. She flipped over so that she faced him and kissed his mouth. She had no patience for the gentle good morning kiss he returned to her. She pressed herself against him and kissed him passionately. She wanted him.

Hannibal returned her kiss and rose, taking her in his arms. He dwarfed her like a lion with a gazelle, but she was no gazelle. A thrill shot through her as he ran his hands along the curve of her breast and down her waist to her thigh. Her breath hitched as he nipped gently at her bottom lip and then slid his mouth to her neck.

She arched her back, angling toward him as he entered her, and they moved in time with each other, building slowly, deliciously, to climax.

"Daddy!" a child called. Little footsteps pattered outside their room a second before their door burst open.

Sophonisba stifled the groan that threatened to escape her lips as she wrapped a fur around her. *Right when it was getting good.* She put a protective hand over her belly as she turned from her husband to face the door of the bedroom.

Hannibal tied a robe around his waist.

Four-year-old Hamilcar pushed open the door, beaming with excitement for the new day.

Hannibal glanced at her with a mix of exasperation and pride. She knew the feeling.

The child ran to their bed and jumped up on it, lunging to hug both parents at once.

"Hamilcar," Hannibal said. He smiled, his face brightening as he grabbed the child, tossed him high into the air, and set him back on the ground next to the bed.

Sophonisba looked at her son disapprovingly. "You're much too old to come into your father's bed. Go. Wash his sandals and get ready for breakfast."

Hamilcar turned to Hannibal as if his father might have a more desirable response. His course black curls soared over his head like birds flapping in the breeze, and his eyes were full of hope.

Hannibal's face turned to stone. The discussion was over. She bit back a smile and struggled to keep her own face hard.

Hamilcar's little shoulders sagged. He turned and ran from the room.

As soon as the door closed, Sophonisba turned to face her husband, putting her hands on his bare, muscled chest and pressing her lips against his collarbone, ready to pick up where they had left off.

Hannibal kissed her cheek and instead moved away from the bed. He grabbed his tunic. "The day is half over," he said.

Disappointed, she reached out to run her hand along his arm. "I have a surprise for you."

He grinned at her, his eyes dipping down her body and

then back to her face. He winked. "It might have to wait."

Sophonisba leaned back in the bed and brought her hands to her belly. She held his eyes. "I think it's a little girl."

His hand stilled on the belt he had wrapped around his tunic. His eyes widened and dipped down her body once again, slower this time, taking in her still-flat stomach. When he sought her eyes again, his face was lit with pride.

The bed sagged as he sat next to her and put his hand where hers rested on her middle. He kissed her lips gently.

"This is good news," he said.

She leaned into him, and his arms went around her.

Something shattered against the tiled floor downstairs.

Hannibal stood, and Sophonisba sighed. She hoped little Hamilcar's baby sister wouldn't be quite so hard on the ceramics.

Hannibal finished tying his belt. As he left the room, he glanced over his shoulder at her and winked.

CHAPTER 7

Barca Front Hall, Carthage

Hannibal descended the stairs to the front hall in time to see Lady Barca and Hasdrubal receiving a letter from a messenger. Hasdrubal opened the missive and scanned it while Lady Barca looked over his shoulder. They both looked up as they saw him. Something was wrong.

"What news?" Hannibal asked.

"Word from Iberia," his mother said. She studied him for any sign that things might not be as bad as she thought. The crease between her eyebrows only deepened.

"You may leave," Hannibal said to the messenger, who hovered in the hall as though waiting for a breakfast invitation. *Nosy messengers.*

The messenger fled the compound, gone by the time Hannibal's foot hit the tiled floor of the great hall.

Iberia. He had so many memories of his father in Iberia. They had founded the city of Akra-Leuka together, watching it grow from a settlement to a commercial hub. The bricks of her city shone like gold in the sun. There might have been other cities had their Ebro campaign been successful. He ought to have known. He pressed his lips together. Blaming himself forever wouldn't avenge his father's death.

Hasdrubal handed him the letter and he took it, feeling his pulse thrum with dread at the words on the page. After his father's death, the city's defense was entirely on his shoulders.

Hasdrubal grabbed the map of Iberia from the map chest and flattened it on the table. His thin fingers traced the region, resting on Saguntum. "Romans have crossed the Ebro and laid siege to Saguntum. The city's most likely fallen by now," he said. His handsome features furrowed in concentration and trepidation.

"Under the treaty, Saguntum belongs to Carthage," Hannibal said, looking up from the letter and meeting his brother's gaze. If the Romans were breaking the peace treaty that had ended the last war, they must want another one. Saguntum was just the beginning.

Hannibal walked over to the map that Hasdrubal pointed to. After a brief pause, he said, "Ready a dozen maniples to leave at once. We'll join with the garrison at Cartagena and converge on Saguntum to the north."

"The Council will convene tomorrow," Lady Barca said. "Let us wait for the process of law."

Hannibal glanced at her to indicate that he had heard her. He understood that her intent was to keep peace between the clans, but he knew that this was too sensitive of a problem to wait for the Council to make up its mind. Even Ida Hanna had to see that.

His mind ran fast with calculations. Carthage needed Iberia. Trade with Iberia was the reason she prospered. The riches Carthage brought home from Iberian mines were enough to fight Rome for the territory, but it also brought in a large percentage of Carthage's food supply. Not to mention, letting Rome take Saguntum was bad precedent and worse policy, since Rome had proven her endless hunger. If Saguntum fell, all of Iberia was next, and Carthage would follow. Hannibal wouldn't let that happen.

An attack on Saguntum that was sanctioned by the Council would be seen by the Romans as a deliberate attack on Rome and a declaration of war. By launching it without the Council's permission, he would allow Carthage to respond in might on the battlefield while allowing the Council the ability to condemn it if Rome sent a delegation. It was a risky maneuver since the Hannas might very well hand Hannibal over to the Romans in order to maintain the façade of peace. But Ida knew as well as Hannibal did that Iberia was imperative to the infrastructure of their city. Enemies are stacked upon layers. Upon the right layer, one finds an ally.

Hannibal was not going to stand by and let this happen. He was in command and it was his duty to vanquish the Romans. It had been his father's wish in life and in death, and Hannibal couldn't fail him now that opportunity arose.

"We leave at once," he said. He watched his mother's face darken and directed his gaze to his brother, who looked eager for a chance at war. "Rome will argue that if we respond, it's a breach of treaty."

"They can argue that," Hasdrubal said. "But it doesn't make sense. They breached the treaty first. Either they have voided the treaty or we are rectifying its terms."

"They can argue whatever they want if it's war they're after. They can say that Saguntum became their ally of its own free will."

"But they weren't Rome's ally when the treaty was signed," Hasdrubal said. "Doesn't that count for something? Never mind that true allies are rarely put to siege before the alliance is struck."

Hannibal studied his younger brother, over-eager to see the battlefield. Still, he was right. Rome had no business encroaching on Carthage's western frontier. "We must meet aggression with strength. I will gladly die for every inch of our soil they have trod."

Hasdrubal's face relaxed. "I'll make arrangements for daybreak tomorrow. Should I arrange for your family?"

Hannibal looked up at the door leading to his quarters, where Sophonisba was undoubtedly coaxing breakfast into Hamilcar's mouth while he chattered at her rapidly about his father's big horses or the latest pebble he picked up in the street. "Yes," Hannibal said. "Mother, will you represent us at Council?"

"I don't like it," she said.

Hannibal took her hand. "I don't either."

She pursed her lips. "Promise me you will return."

"We'll catch them by surprise. They'll never know we're coming."

It wasn't the promise she wanted, but she nodded.

CHAPTER 8

Outside Carthage

A train of wagons holding supplies for the journey curved around a hill west of Carthage. Horses and soldiers rode along the shore, away from the city. From his mount, Hannibal glanced behind him, taking in the spires of the watchtowers and the pink glow of the early morning sun on the white city walls.

When would he next return to his city? When Hamilcar Barca had left Carthage that day, had he known that he would never return home?

Hannibal had relived the fateful moment a thousand times. The rush of the river current. The shouts of the Sacred Band uttered and cut short by the water. The clunk of a weapon hitting a submerged shield. And somehow, above the roar of men and water, the splitting sound of an arrow breaking flesh. His father's eyes had turned upon him one last time, glowing with pride and death. Then the Barca shield had smashed into his skull.

Hannibal blinked hard and focused his eyes on the yucca plants lining the road and the hot sun on his hands. Still, his thoughts strayed from the present. This was the first campaign he would lead without his father in command. He wondered if he would even be here now if he had avenged his father's death instead of allowing the Council to send another peace delegation and make diplomatic niceties.

Those were futile thoughts. He turned his attention to the stream of soldiers riding along ahead of him. The trip that stretched before them was full of too many unknowns for Hannibal's liking. By the time they made it to Saguntum, would there be anything left of the city to save? Would the Romans be waiting for them? Would they be outnumbered? Certainly with access to the silver mines near Saguntum, the Romans would have already turned quite a profit from their little game.

Hannibal hung toward the back of the trail beside his family's covered wagon. Inside, Sophonisba rode with their son. Perhaps he should have left them at home with his mother. He smiled, imagining how she wouldn't have stood for it. He admired her stubborn streak. It was one of the many things he loved about her. Some years down the road, she would take Lady Barca's place in the household.

Hamilcar stuck his head out of the wagon, grinning and waving at his father. He leaned further over the wagon's edge and pointed to Hannibal's horse. He giggled gleefully. The horses never failed to delight the child. The laughter raised Hannibal's spirits.

The wagon hit a bump in the road and jostled Hamilcar against the side.

Hannibal frowned at him and shook his head slightly. He heard Sophonisba's muffled voice telling the child to sit.

Hamilcar saluted to his father before pulling his body and head safely back inside the wagon.

CHAPTER 9

Cartagena

Sophonisba stood at the top of one of Cartagena's turrets. The night was balmy, but still she shivered. This wasn't the desert. The humidity wet her skin, and the cool breeze sucked away her body heat. Torchlight flickered above her, casting ominous shadows around her. She looked out over the green plains of Iberia and down at the empty, dark wall that surrounded the city.

All at once, a gate opened in the wall and dark figures poured into the field.

She squinted, seeing her husband and his brother mounted at their lead. Hannibal didn't glance behind him as he rode away, but she hadn't expected him to. He wouldn't have seen her in the darkness even if he had.

The convoy raced away, charging into the dark wilderness ahead. Sophonisba's eyes followed them for as far as she could see, until the dark figures at the front of the army became too blurry to pick out.

She lifted her gaze to the place where flames stroked the northeastern horizon. The march to Saguntum had seemed so long to her earlier in the day, when Hannibal had told her of it, but now, looking out at the glow that brightened the night and dimmed the stars, the march seemed far too short. The army galloped toward the burning city as swiftly as their horses could carry them.

Sophonisba shivered. Hannibal had told her that he had a plan, and it was a good one. She had felt confident that it would work a few short hours ago, but now she shook her head. She was still confident, she told herself. It would work.

She had prayed that the gods would protect Hannibal, and now she hoped that they would see fit to grant her request. For now, she was powerless. She tightened her hands into fists. She would have to trust that her husband's good instincts would carry him safely back to her. She would fight her own battle until he came home.

CHAPTER 10

Outside Saguntum

Nightfall shrouded the army as Hannibal led his troops to a point fifty yards in front of Saguntum's wall. A line of rubble showed precisely how far the catapults could reach, and they stayed just beyond. The smell of smoke hung heavy in the air. He surveyed the still burning city.

His soldiers stood silently, waiting for his command. His Sacred Band surrounded him, looking to him for directions. He had told no one but Sophonisba about his plan of attack, and although she had feigned ignorance, he could read her face. But the plan had changed since last night; he'd only finished working out the final details as they had marched the last leg of the journey. He felt the familiar calm of a solid strategy replace any agitation from the journey.

Maherbal, the captain of the Sacred Band, stood at Hannibal's side. His features were angular and sharp. His eyes showed a ruthless loyalty that terrified his enemies. He was a bony man, which gave the appearance of weakness to many foes before they fell to his lanky dexterity. Hannibal knew that if backed into a corner, Maherbal wouldn't hesitate to gouge out a man's eyes and strangle him with his bare hands in order to preserve the General's life.

"The men await your orders, General," Hasdrubal said, his voice barely above a whisper. His horse shifted slightly under him at the sound of his voice.

"Have the men pretend to set up camp," Hannibal said. The authority of his tone brought confidence to the faces of his guards, and they stood straighter. "From the walls of Saguntum, they'll see us digging in for the night."

"And then?" Hasdrubal asked.

Hannibal turned to Maherabal. "Find me the smallest member of the Sacred Band."

Without a word, Maherabal disappeared into the night.

Hasdrubal's face contorted with confusion. "What are we doing?"

Hannibal met his gaze and held it for a moment. A light went off in Hasdrubal's head.

"The water drain?" he asked.

"The Romans might control the city, but they didn't build it," Hannibal said. Adrenaline coursed through his veins, tensing his muscles and dilating his pupils. He was in control, and he expected this to work. If the Roman guards spotted the army setting up camp for the night, they wouldn't expect an attack until dawn. The only flaw was if the Romans acted immediately.

Maherabal returned with a slender Sacred Band guard, barely more than a boy, who looked equal parts eager and terrified.

Hannibal dismounted and placed his hand on the guard's shoulder. The young man looked into his pupils and his fright vanished, as if a current of electric strength ran from lion to cub. The rest of the Sacred Band circled them to hear Hannibal's strategy.

"If you listen carefully and do as I say, you will lead your brothers to victory before daybreak," Hannibal said.

"Yes, General," the young guard said. He shifted his weight in anticipation.

Hannibal pointed to a small creek running behind the Carthaginian line, barely discernible in the dark. "That creek drains from the streets of Saguntum. Remove the grate and follow the water line past the city walls. Kill any man who stands between you and the front gate. Your brothers will be waiting outside of the gate for you to open it."

The slender guard nodded, and he slipped away to the creek. He looked back and met Hannibal's eyes. The ferocity, the energy. It filled the boy up as he turned into the darkness.

Hannibal's eyes followed the darkness. "Maherabal, lead your men to the wall from the cover of the eastern woods," he paused to let the direction sink in. "If one lookout sees you, all is lost. We'll follow with reinforcements once the gate is opened."

Maherabal's rich, solemn voice said, "The city is yours, General." He saluted and led his men back behind the Carthaginian line.

CHAPTER 11

Before the Walls of Saguntum

In Maherabal's mind, nothing in the history of man existed outside of this plan. He led the Sacred Band along the dark shadows between the eastern woods and the city walls. Their black armor was silent as they crept forward. One clink, one stumble, and he knew that the entire army would perish. They shuffled in a single file line along the wall until they reached the front gate. There they waited, still mute.

Maherabal didn't so much as inhale. He and his men could have been mistaken for statues in a courtyard. They were so still that each man was a just shadow in the dark, dewy night.

Moments after they arrived, the door to the gate cracked open, creaking and spilling shouts into the night air.

Maherabal grabbed the door and flung it wide, revealing the slender guard staggering backward in victory. He had a sword lodged in his abdomen, and his mouth struggled to form words.

A group of Roman guards shouted and raised their swords at the sight of the Sacred Band squinting into the city gate. One Roman turned from them and shouted.

He's calling backup, Maherabal thought.

One of the Romans shoved the slender guard to the ground, shouting at him as he fell. The young man's eyes were wide. He slid across the ground as a Roman foot slammed into his side. He didn't cry out in pain. Only garbled words tumbled from his mouth, along with dark red blood.

The Roman's livid gaze met Maherabal's with a dare.

The sight of his fallen comrade boiled Maherabal's gut with bloodlust and fury. He struck first, slashing the Roman to the ground. The Sacred Band followed him, pouring into the city and vanquishing the guards. More Roman soldiers poured into the streets. A few looked ready to fight, but many more wore faces of curious sleep, inquiring about the source of the commotion.

Maherabal's lone purpose in this moment was to slay Roman soldiers. He dodged swords and fists, slashing through red cloaks and white faces. Romans fell one after another. He ran his sword through a Roman's chest, twisting out a scream. He yanked his sword free, and the sharp blade slid out with sickening ease, already trained on its next victim.

Blood flew as the Sacred Band inflicted ten deaths to every scratch of their own.

CHAPTER 12

Outside Saguntum

Hannibal watched from afar as the main gate of Saguntum was opened and the Carthaginian elite burst into the unsuspecting city. Hasdrubal stood next to him, antsy to join them in battle.

It was time.

"Take our city!" Hannibal shouted.

Ready for the command, the army abandoned the faux camp of light sheets and set a quick pace toward the city.

Hannibal led his army through the front gate. Bodies in red uniforms littered the ground in pools of blood, as if the fabric of their tunics had been liquefied around them. The Sacred Band had spread out across the city square to finish off any cowards lurking in the shadows. The battle was already won.

Maherabal emerged from the guardhouse beside the front gate and met Hannibal's eyes.

"General," he said, "This way, sir."

Hannibal dismounted and followed Maherabal into the building. Hasdrubal followed.

Inside, a torch burned along the wall, beating back the

shadows. A ranking Roman officer struggled against the binding that held him in his chair. Blood flowed from a gash in his cheek, his nose, and his lip. Bruising around his left eye was dark against his pale skin. A red drip hung from his chin. He tried to swipe at it with his shoulder.

A member of the Sacred Band punched him hard in the face again. "Tell us!" the soldier of the Sacred Band shouted.

The Roman officer turned his head away and spoke only in Latin, which awarded him another hit in the jaw. Most Carthaginians didn't speak Latin, and the officer knew it. He would fight his battle by feigning cluelessness.

Hannibal shook his head at the scene before him. This would not work. He looked to Maherabal.

"He's unresponsive," Maherabal said.

Hannibal walked up to the Roman officer, staring fiercely at the Roman until he noticed Hannibal's presence in front of him. "I'm prepared to accept your surrender," Hannibal said.

The Roman's face contorted and he spit in Hannibal's direction. The phlegm fell short of Hannibal's feet. In Latin, the Roman shouted, "I surrendered with honor, dog. Is this how you barbarians treat an officer?"

Hannibal's face didn't so much as twitch at the words, though he understood them perfectly. What an odious chore it had been to learn the language of the enemy, but his father had insisted. He switched to Latin. "Please do not yell," he said.

Hearing his own tongue from the lips of a Carthaginian seemed to enrage the officer further. He renewed his struggle against the ropes that bound him, twisting until the chair rocked. "Imbeciles! The rogue bastards of Africa! Uncivilized murderers with no respect for the codes of war!"

Hannibal's anger boiled over. He smacked the officer hard across the jaw, sending blood and teeth flying and tipping the chair back so far that it almost toppled the rest of the way. His words came from his mouth like lashes. "Codes of war? What of peace treaties? I will not honor the surrender of a traitor to our contract."

"I am a soldier. I follow orders and report to my—"

"I have a report for you to deliver." With a flick of his wrist, Hannibal flung his dagger from his belt into the base of the Roman officer's throat. "Go home," he said.

Blood spurted from the wound. The soldier's eyes bugged out and then were screened by the glassy haze of death. He fell over sideways in his chair and slouched until the rope bindings caught his limp body.

Hannibal turned and exited the guardhouse, using his anger to propel him as he climbed the city walls alone. Codes of war! These Romans knew nothing of the codes of war, or they would not have come. This wasn't about codes. It was about greed.

At the top of the wall, he extinguished the torchlight that hung nearby and stared up at the expanse of the stars above him. What prophetic words were the gods writing on the heavens for him tonight?

A cool breeze licked his face, bringing with it the fragrance of ashes and earth. The cool of the night slowed his pulse and quieted his rage.

He said, "Illuminate your prophecy to me. Will this battle end here? Will the gods reward Carthage in victory?" He waited and watched. Even after tonight's sound victory, he hardly dared hope that the future would bring equally sound victories for Carthage.

He gazed up at the sky, watching, waiting for the relationships between the stars to become clear to him. The gods didn't speak quickly. They didn't need to; they had all of time at their fingertips.

He breathed deeply of the acrid, smoky air as he searched for the lion constellation, the stars that represented Carthage. He found it dimmed around the light of the full moon.

A long moment passed, and a shadow crept across the face of the moon, swallowing it until the moon was nothing more than a faint ring of light with a blackened middle. The lion was gone, snuffed out by the fading moon.

The lion of Carthage will be snuffed out until all that remains is the memory of her glory. The words came unbidden to Hannibal's mind. He longed to doubt them. He wished he could be ignorant with his men in Saguntum, reveling in the night's victory.

He shook his head. The gods had spoken, but he could have misinterpreted their words. For the sake of Carthage, he dearly hoped so.

CHAPTER 13

The Council Chamber, Carthage

Lady Barca watched a guard open the doors to the council chamber. White robes emerged between the heavy doors, led by the Roman Senator, Fabius Maximus. His white hair rivaled the white of his robe, and the wart above his upper lip perfectly punctuated the smugness in his eyes.

Lady Barca pressed her lips together. A delegation so soon was proof that Rome meant to go to war. Was there any way to avoid it?

Sapanibal shifted in her seat, and Lady Barca put a hand on her daughter's leg to still her.

She counted Romans as they traipsed down the half dozen stone stairs into the chamber. There were eight of them. No doubt more waited outside the room. She was glad now that at least the Council could say with honesty that they had not issued the attack on Saguntum.

Ida Hanna followed Lady Barca's gaze, and his expression turned lethal at the sight of the Romans. Layers of enemies. At the look of his face, the rest of the Council turned to behold the Romans. Tension climbed high and thick around them. Mutters filled the room, echoing off the walls. The mutters escalated to heckles and shouts as the Romans reached the front of the room and stood before the Council.

The only ones in the room, besides Lady Barca, who maintained their composure were Geromachus, an elder of the Council, and Massinissa, the handsome young King of Numidia, whose father had served in the last war against Rome with General Hamilcar. Hannibal's marriage to the daughter of Numidia's most powerful senator had only strengthened the alliance.

Lady Barca stood. Sapanibal resumed her squirming, her eyes wide with confusion. Lady Barca flicked her eyes back to the Romans, refusing to give in to the nerves that swirled in her stomach. She hated not knowing if her sons were safe or if their counter attack on Saguntum had gone according to plan. Was the presence of the Romans here evidence that it had? They could just as easily foretell horrible news. She did some quick math. No, there was no way this delegation could have heard about the attack before leaving Rome. They must have assumed Carthage would fight back.

Ida stood for the Hannas but kept shouting loud insults. He cursed Rome and its delegation, pouring fuel on the hate fire that pulsed throughout the room.

Lady Barca hated the Romans at least as much as Ida Hanna, but she held her tongue. By the look on Maximus's face, the Carthaginian Council's aggravation pleased him.

Her eyes slid along the Roman figures. Maximus was the oldest at nearly sixty. His robe bore the signature purple stripes of a Roman senator. All of the Romans looked to him, though three others also wore the stripes.

A young man also accompanied the delegation. Lady Barca fixed her eyes on him. *What's his purpose?* she wondered. He looked even younger than her sons. While the other Romans were smug, his face held reserve.

"Guards, throw them out in the street!" Ida shouted. His face was red, and his fists pounded the tabletop in front of him vigorously. He had completely lost control of his temper.

"Here to tell more Roman lies!" another member of the Council yelled.

Maximus raised his hand for quiet, but the noise in the chamber instead grew more deafening with the thunder of venomous insults and table pounding.

"Let them be heard," Lady Barca said. Her calm, feminine tone cut through the male racket. She waited while the Council members quieted.

Ida glared at her. The others looked at her with trepidation.

"Let them be heard," she repeated when the room was quiet.

The youngest Roman looked at her with interest. His eyes met hers for the briefest of flashes before Maximus spoke up with an air of Roman arrogance.

"I come as the voice of the Roman Senate and the people of Rome. Your brash attack on Saguntum has caused grave concern."

Lady Barca felt some relief at this statement. If Maximus was concerned about the attack, then it must have gone in Carthage's favor. Perhaps the advantage was theirs.

Ida interrupted. "You broke the treaty line of the Ebro River."

"We were invited to Saguntum by the elders of the city.

They swore allegiance to Rome," Maximus said. His voice dipped low.

"Rome found silver in Saguntum's mines and bribed their allegiance to get to their wealth," Ida snapped.

Murmurs of agreement rippled through the Council.

"That's enough," Lady Barca said.

Ida clamped his mouth shut, but his jawbone pulsed.

Lady Barca was irritated by Roman politics and loopholes too, but provoking the Senator wouldn't solve the problem. Then again, maybe it didn't matter what she said.

Maximus spoke again. "Your barbaric retaliation and murder of Roman soldiers cannot go unnoticed. Rome seeks to avoid a war, yet a simple matter for diplomacy has been blown into a deafening call for war from Carthage."

Lady Barca raised her eyebrows a fraction and kept her voice cool and level. "This is the first of diplomacy this chamber has heard since the treaty that ended our last war."

The Carthaginians in the chamber again murmured their agreement. Lady Barca watched Ida's skinny nose flair with fury and noted several fists clenched in laps, but the Council remained quiet and let her speak for them.

"Saguntum was not Rome's ally at the time of that treaty," she said, "and forming such an alliance now is in blatant disregard to the treaty. Not to mention that we heard a Roman siege was required to procure such an alliance."

Nods rippled down the line of Council members.

Maximus lifted his chin imperiously, refusing to acknowledge Lady Barca's words. He held his arm out from his side. His hand grasped the end of his robe, creating a large, visible fold, which he gestured to as he spoke. "The people of Rome offer this chamber a somber choice. In the fold of my robe, I hold the choice of war or peace."

Ida pounded his fist on the table. "It seems that the Senate of Rome has already decided that question," he snapped.

Maximus's face turned stony. "I repeat that I offer Carthage this choice."

Like the building of a storm, the chamber air filled with tension. The members of the Council glanced around at each other and then rested their gaze on Lady Barca.

Maximus, too, fixed his eyes on her.

Her heart thrummed in her throat, but she met his gaze with a steely stare of resolve. She lifted her chin slightly. "Isn't it Rome's choice?" she said.

Maximus's eyes shrank to slits. "War!" he said. He dropped the folds of his robe from his hand with a zealous flare from his wild eyes.

The chamber erupted, some shouting protests and some making livid death threats. The guards standing near the entrance to the council chamber surrounded the delegation. More Carthaginian soldiers poured into the room at the shouts of war and grabbed the Romans.

"Scipio!" one of the Roman senators shouted.

In response, the youngest Roman unsheathed his sword, preparing for the worst. He glanced at Lady Barca, and she was struck by the lack of hate and zeal that she saw in his expression. He was a man bound by duty. Unlike the other Roman dogs before her, she couldn't help but respect him. Did that make her disloyal? No. She would give her homeland everything she had, but she would betray herself if she couldn't recognize an admirable man when she saw one. It was too bad he was a Roman.

Before the situation escalated beyond control, Lady Barca commanded, "Let them live to tell Rome of the war they have chosen."

Ida protested loudly. "I say slay them all now and shorten the war."

Sapanibal gasped and grabbed Lady Barca's robe, as though this would somehow give her reassurance or protection.

"The code of war will be upheld in this chamber," Lady Barca said.

"We are the codes," Ida said.

Lady Barca saw the hatred in his eyes and knew that he meant it. The thought sickened her. "At the end of a war, at the end of a life, all we have left is our honor. No one will say that Carthage is without honor."

Ida glared at her. "And without honor, that life might never have to end."

"All lives end. I assure you."

Ida's eyes bored into Lady Barca's for several taut seconds before he slammed his fists on the table and relented.

The guards unhanded the Romans and let them leave, shutting the council room doors loudly behind them.

The members of the Council jumped to the council floor to volunteer themselves for battle.

Ida stood and tried to take charge of the room from Lady Barca. "Conscript the army," he said. "Call for mercenaries from our African allies. Where are our friends from Numidia?"

Massinissa stood and turned to Lady Barca. "The horses

of Numidia owe an eternal debt to Carthage and the valor of Hamilcar Barca. We will ride at once."

Lady Barca nodded in acceptance, satisfied with the young king's answer and demeanor. She noted that Sapanibal seemed suddenly very interested in the meeting, and an idea of a different nature took shape.

The chamber descended into blood-curdling yells for death in battle, and the room again echoed with ear-splitting shrieks. As Ida led the patriotic call, Lady Barca took Sapanibal's arm and slipped through the raging men out the back door.

Lady Barca saw her daughter look behind her and catch the stare of the dashing Massinissa. He smiled at her, interest lighting his midnight features, and Sapanibal stood straighter and offered him her coyest smile.

The gods themselves could not have kept Rome from declaring war on Carthage, yet Lady Barca allowed herself a brief moment of satisfaction; Massinissa would make for a useful political ally for the Barca family and for Carthage if she played this right.

CHAPTER 14

The Barca Compound,
Later the Same Evening

Lady Barca sat in her chamber inside the house going over the household accounts. Though she appeared serene, her mind was still racing from the events of this afternoon and the implications.

A knock sounded at her door and a servant entered. "You have a guest," the servant said. "He's waiting for you in the front hall."

Lady Barca arrived in the front hall in time to see King Massinissa tracing his finger along the polished wood of the chest that housed the maps of the known world. His brow was furrowed, and he wet his lips with his tongue once, then twice.

Lady Barca hadn't expected him to come calling tonight, but she was not surprised.

He glanced up and pulled his hand away from the map chest, clasping it in front of him. His dark, elegant features showed energy and hope when he saw her enter, as if he had half expected her to send him away.

"King Massinissa, Carthage appreciates your support, but

there are many pressing needs of our household with war on the horizon," she said, choosing her words carefully and keeping her tone even.

"I understand, and I wish no burden on you or your household in this most urgent of hours," he said. His intelligent eyes remained steady on hers. He wet his lips again, this time looking more confident.

"Yet you are here," she said.

"My family has always been loyal to Carthage, and to the Barcas most especially. I wish to grant your favor in arranging a close alliance between our families."

"What do you propose?" she asked, keeping her face neutral.

"I propose a marriage. I would make Sapanibal my queen so that we may link our families for the future." He paused, studying her expression for any hint of what she was thinking.

Lady Barca nodded, hiding her satisfaction. It would do no good to let on that this had been her intention as well.

"Sapanibal!" Lady Barca called.

As if she had been waiting for her mother's call, Sapanibal emerged on the balcony above the front hall. She beamed nervously at the king below her. No doubt she understood little but that she was to marry a handsome king, and she did little to conceal her glee.

Lady Barca sighed at her daughter's naïveté, remembering her own childish excitement when her parents announced that she was to marry Hamilcar Barca. She had learned her duties eventually. Sapanibal would too. Lady Barca would try to explain things to her later, though she doubted her daughter would listen. Sapanibal was a good daughter with a sweet disposition, but she lived in a dream world much of the time, a strange trait for a Barca, to be sure.

Lady Barca continued, "Sapanibal, once the war has ended, you will be betrothed to King Massinissa and become Queen of Numidia."

Sapanibal, doing her best to repress her excitement and not quite succeeding, bowed her head slightly. "As you wish."

"Does this please you?" the king asked her, turning his eyes on her.

Pleasure washed her features. "Very much so."

"Then it is settled," Lady Barca said.

"I will ride at once to meet your sons in Iberia," Massinissa said. He stole a glance at Sapanibal before sharply turning and exiting the house.

When he was gone, Lady Barca shot a look at her daughter. "You betray too much, Sapanibal. Men will take as much as you give them. You must practice restraint to receive respect."

"I have no need for such politics," Sapanibal said. She vanished behind the curtain inside the balcony, off to dream of being a great African queen adored by all and doted on by her royal husband.

Lady Barca sighed. War was coming. The girl would grow up soon enough. Perhaps she should allow one last youthful fantasy.

CHAPTER 15

Saguntum

Whereas the banquet halls in Carthage were whitewashed and tiled and glowing with candlelight hung along the walls, the hall in Saguntum featured wood beams spanning the ceilings, and from the center beams hung chandeliers that were flaming with the light of a hundred candles each.

The hall burst with Carthaginian soldiers feasting their stomach on wild meat and Iberian wine, and their eyes took in the beauty of the Saguntine women who served them. Voices rumbled through the room with frenzied excitement. Lutes played festive music from the back corner of the hall and silverware clanked against porcelain and wood.

In the middle of the room, three men who were drunk on wine thumped their feet and grabbed at each other's backsides in a strange dance that flattered no one. Two more men joined them, looping arms and swinging each other until they ran into a nearby table. Wine spilled on the tabletop, and a spoon clattered on the floor.

"More wine!" someone called, and a busty serving woman with glistening black hair brought another jug of wine to the table. One of the dancing men grabbed her hands as she turned to walk away from the table and pulled her into his made up jig.

All the male eyes around her clamped their gazes to her bouncing breasts and catcalled into the fray.

Hannibal sat at the head table, opposite the lute orchestra, wishing that his mood matched the celebration around him. The sign from the gods refused to be shaken from his thoughts, and his wine glass was the only one in the room still untouched.

Hasdrubal and Maherabal sat on either side of him.

Hasdrubal gulped the entire contents of his glass and slammed it down on the table with a loud bang. "More wine," he said. He grinned wildly at Hannibal and elbowed him until Hannibal forced a smile.

A full-figured Saguntine woman approached the table with a ceramic wine bottle and red grapes. She filled Hasdrubal's glass and offered some to Maherabal, looking at him with the sparkle of lust in her eyes.

"I'm not interested in wine," Maherabal said, returning her look.

"What interests you, Captain?" she said, her brows arching deliciously.

"The company of a beautiful woman," he said. He had a way of saying exactly what he wanted. He had a way of effortlessly getting it, too.

"Only one?" Her lips pursed flirtatiously. She winked, seductively feeding herself a grape off of the vine. She turned and walked away, looking over shoulder at him.

Maherabal stood from the table. "Permission to retire for the evening, General," he said to Hannibal.

"Enjoy that Iberian woman while you can, Maherabal. You'll have to settle for an Italian before long," Hannibal said.

"It will be my civic duty," Maherabal said.

Despite his solemn mood, Hannibal couldn't help but smirk. With drunken revelry all around them, Maherabal was dutiful, even in pleasure.

Hasdrubal leaned over to Maherabal. "Go already, b'fore she finds someone else." He laughed loudly and waggled his eyebrows, insinuating that he might go to her himself.

Maherabal disappeared immediately, hot on the scent of the Saguntine woman.

Hasdrubal slammed back another glass of wine.

"Thirsty as a fish, brother?" Hannibal asked him. He was only partially joking.

"S'not my fault you don' know how to party," Hasdrubal's words slurred, and he swayed back in his seat a little. "You wouldn't know how to party even if we killed all the Romans in the world."

"When we have killed them all, I assure you, I will be drunker than you and will run naked through all of Carthage announcing my victory."

"This I want to see," Hasdrubal said.

Hannibal picked up his wine glass and stood.

The soldiers in the hall snapped to quiet attention, their eyes on their victorious General.

"A drink to the men in this hall!" Hannibal said. "Our blades may be rusty, but they cut Roman flesh all the same!"

The hall roared with guttural shouts of agreement. Every soldier tipped his glass in the air.

Still standing, Hannibal threw back his wine in one giant

gulp and slammed his cup down in front of Hasdrubal.

"You spend all night writing that speech? You should write it down so it can be studied," Hasdrubal said. He clapped his hands mockingly and then slapped his thighs at his own joke.

"I will return to Cartagena in the morning," Hannibal said, hoping his brother was sober enough to remember. "Leave a garrison here, but bring the army back tomorrow."

Hasdrubal nodded, and the two clasped their hands together in the customary Carthaginian handshake. "Expecting a war?" he asked. For a moment, the merriness left his eyes and was replaced by a flash of worry.

Hannibal said. "A war has begun. It is ours to finish."

Hasdrubal nodded. Then he put his smile back on. "Then we'd better do all our carousing tonight."

Hannibal pressed his lips together. Sometimes he envied his brother's ability to live in the moment and forget about the future. It was something he'd never had a chance to learn. Hasdrubal envied his experiences with their father and the fact that Hannibal was now the general, but he would never know what Hannibal had sacrificed for the role he must play.

CHAPTER 16

Cartagena

The following morning, before the sun had risen, Hannibal galloped into Cartagena with Maherabal and a dozen other members of the Sacred Band. When they arrived at the entrance to the city, the gates opened and then dropped quickly behind them once they had entered. A stationed guard took Hannibal's reins as he dismounted.

"What news from Carthage of our victory?" Hannibal asked.

The guard responded, "A Roman delegation was expected in Carthage two days ago, but we have not received word from the Council."

He was unsurprised but frustrated nonetheless. A delegation from Rome could only mean war. Would the Romans have traveled so far so quickly for peace? Unlikely.

He went inside the general's quarters and saw Sophonisba curled in bed. Hamilcar was snuggled into her stomach, wrapped in blankets, and both breathed the slow, steady breaths of sleep.

Hannibal quietly removed his armor and tunic and sat on the edge of the bed, looking at his wife and wishing he didn't have to wake her and tell her of his decision. He ran his fingers through her thick, black hair and traced a finger down her cheek.

Her eyes opened. "I didn't hear the horns," she whispered. Sleep still crouched in her eyes.

"The army will be back by dusk. I came early."

"You come early when you know you'll be leaving soon," she said. The sleep fell away, and she raised herself on one elbow, careful not to wake Hamilcar.

"I expect news from Carthage today," he said.

"Surely the Romans can't have gotten here so quickly. You only just attacked."

"They want war, and they knew what it would take to provoke us. This isn't over," Hannibal said. He kissed her face and worried, not for the first time, what war could do to his wife and children. He had to send them as far from the battlefield as he could. "You will take Hamilcar back to Carthage. My mother will protect you until this is done."

Sophonisba shot upright in bed, drawing her knees to her chest and pulling away from Hannibal. Her eyes flashed with anger and hurt. "We came here for you. Why would you send us away?"

He reached for her hand, hating himself for offending her and hoping he could make her understand how much he loved her and how many deaths he would die before anything happened to her. "It will be an ugly, brutal war," he said. "I can't let you stay with me."

"Why not? Are you afraid I can't handle it?" Her defiant words stung.

"I'm afraid I can't handle it," he said.

A little of the fury drained from her face, and she clasped his hand tightly. "It's going to be fine," she said. "You're going to be the brilliant general who leads Carthage to victory and squashes Rome completely."

The image of the moon disappearing behind a great shadow still replayed itself in his mind. "I saw the stars the other night and again last night. The war is only beginning. I will lose many soldiers. This war may spell the end for Carthage."

Sophonisba looked down at their hands. Hannibal's eyes followed her gaze. He knew that she didn't hold the omens from the stars in as high of regard as he did.

"Is it possible that you misunderstood?" she asked.

He sighed. "I've been asking myself that over and over, but there's no way. We can only pray for something to shift."

She leaned her head against his shoulder, and they sat in silence for a moment. "I will go with you," she said, looking up at him. Fiery determination lit her eyes.

"No. Please. My worry for you will only weaken me. Please return home. I'm sorry," he said.

Sophonisba opened her mouth to speak, but the words didn't come. The fire in her eyes dimmed. She hesitated for a moment and then pressed herself into Hannibal, her chest arching toward his. She softly kissed him on the mouth and wrapped her arms around his middle. Collapsing into his embrace, she buried her face against his neck.

"Only if you promise not to leave my children without their father," she whispered.

The words pierced his heart, and he held her more tightly. How could he make such a promise?

"I promise," he whispered.

CHAPTER 17

Hannibal's Quarters, Cartagena

Horns blasted from the walls of Cartagena, signifying the return of the army. Hannibal emerged from his quarters at the sound, shaking away the melancholy that had engulfed him all morning at the thought of having to send his family back to Carthage without him. He knew it was the right decision, but he took little solace in that fact. He made his way to the wall above the front gate and watched the approach of Hasdrubal and the troops coming from the north.

A guard announced Hasdrubal's arrival, and Hannibal watched them for a moment. Fifteen thousand soldiers had returned unscathed. He could at least take comfort in the ease of their victory.

Another movement caught his periphery, and he looked to the south. Another army filled the horizon, this one about four times bigger than the army returning from Saguntum. Hannibal squinted, waiting for the figures to become distinguishable. He noted the flag of his own country as well as that of the loyal African mercenaries who had joined in the fight against Rome. Hannibal felt certain that these armies came from Carthage, confirming his suspicions about a war with

Rome.

He saw the commanders from both armies approaching the city gate on horseback and watched the city's guards admit them. If Rome had declared war already, then they needed to settle on strategy.

CHAPTER 18

War Room, Cartagena

Hannibal met the commanders in the war room, a conference room tucked behind a bathhouse along Cartagena's main thoroughfare. Maherabal had ordered them all here on Hannibal's behalf and looked up as the General entered. The scattered conversations halted.

Hannibal looked around at the two dozen or so men seated around the table, pausing as he met the eyes of the Numidian King. Massinissa stood and reached toward Hannibal, clapping him with both arms.

"Massinissa, it is an honor to serve with you again," he said.

"The honor is mine," Massinissa said, keeping a smile in his eyes while his lips remained firm.

Hannibal took his seat. "With an army of fifty thousand, I would assume the word from Carthage is war."

"The Romans left us little choice," Massinissa said. He looked ready to spill the whole story, but Hasdrubal spoke first.

"The Romans will have superior numbers," Hasdrubal said. "What is our strategy?" He directed his gaze to Hannibal, his eyes gleaming with a challenge for his older brother, as if he might at last stump Hannibal and have an opportunity to prove his superiority.

Hannibal was nonplussed. When it came to strategy, Hasdrubal was no match for Hannibal, and they both knew it. "We must strike with stealth. Rome is a giant elephant, which, if given time and space, will trample us all underfoot. We must strike like a lion, without warning."

Hannibal saw the challenge dim in Hasdrubal's eyes at the mention of the lion, and Hannibal knew that he was remembering the lion that had almost devoured him all those years ago. Carthage needed to be like that lion, but better. Hannibal saw a plan forming in his mind's eye and paused, letting the parts come together.

"Are you suggesting a war on Italian soil?" Hasdrubal asked.

The fragments of his idea had not yet settled in his mind and he did not want to disturb them before he could clearly understand and articulate them. Yet the men looked at him expectantly. His words were slow and deliberate. "The Italian people are not Roman. They might welcome our arrival."

Massinissa jumped from his seat and pointed to a map of the world on a wall behind them, gesturing to Greece and Macedonia. "We could request triremes from our ally, Philip of Macedonia. He could transport us to any point in Italy."

"No," Hannibal said. "We would be spotted by the Roman Navy. Their armies would await us on the beach." He didn't add that Philip might not like the idea of going up against a force like Rome, and who could blame him?

Maherabal spoke up. "The Roman navy is large and patrols its waters with precision. Our ships would be lucky to make it to their shores still floating."

Such an attack might have worked fifty years ago, when Carthage still ruled the sea, but now Rome had the best navy in the world.

Hannibal stood and walked around the table to the map. The Romans would expect an invasion by sea, and if they didn't, they would be able to easily avert it before Carthage could bring damage to the pebbles of Rome's shores. No, the sea would not do. He studied the map harder and pointed to Iberia on the map. He swung his hand across the Pyrenees mountain range, the Alps, and finally into Northern Italy. "Our men have always been quick on the march," he said. As he spoke, the plan finally formed in his head.

It took a few moments for his words and gestures to sink in. He looked around the room and watched as one by one the faces lit with shock. Hasdrubal's eyes had gone as wide as if Hannibal was the lion staring him in the face. Maherabal's brow furrowed. Massinissa trailed his finger along the map, tracing the mountainous region Hannibal had pointed out. He looked confused, as if there was something he wasn't understanding that should be obvious.

A Libyan commander stirred from across the table and found his voice. "You want to march an entire army over impassable mountains?" The commander's clothing was made of a lightweight textile from his home in the desert. He sat with his arms hugged close to his chest. Even Cartagena's balmy climate was cooler than he was used to; the mountains would be deadly cold.

Hannibal held the Libyan commander's eyes. "Precisely,"

he said.

The room fell silent, save for the men shifting uncomfortably in their seats. No army had ever passed through those mountains and lived to tell the story. It was insanity.

An Iberian captain cleared his throat. All eyes shifted in his direction. "The mountains are not impassable," he said. "I have guides who have made the trek." His eyes met Hannibal's. "But no army has ever scaled those heights."

Silence followed his words. Hannibal turned the new information over in his mind before speaking. "My army has never tried. I believe we can make the journey in one lunar cycle," he said.

Hasdrubal leaped to his feet. "Are you out of your mind? You want our entire army to scale mountains no army has ever scaled and arrive undetected in Northern Italy in less than thirty days?"

"Should I presume that you have a better plan?" Hannibal asked. He looked around at everyone in the room, daring someone to come up with a better, less risky plan. Hasdrubal sank back to his seat. No one said anything, and he knew they wouldn't. This plan was utter madness, but he had thought through every other strategy there was, and he had come up with nothing else that stood the smallest chance of working. "Madness in time of war is only war," he said. He reclaimed his seat with an air of finality.

After a few beats of skeptical silence, they talked over each other, suggesting ideas to enable this crazy scheme.

CHAPTER 19

Walls of Cartagena

The sun sank in the sky, dipping below the horizon like a god sinking into a bath. Hannibal exited the War Room and approached the city walls to look out at the troops amassed below. Hasdrubal walked alongside him. Neither spoke.

"Hannibal! Hasdrubal!" Massinissa called out behind them as he approached.

Hannibal turned and faced the king.

"I'm optimistic," the king said.

Hannibal nodded, not sure if optimistic was quite the right word.

"It appears that in victory we will also become brothers," the king continued. His face glowed with barely repressed excitement.

Hannibal looked over at Hasdrubal for any hint that his brother understood something he didn't.

Hasdrubal nodded, unsurprised. "Our mother sent us a message of the betrothal," Hasdrubal said. "You are certainly worthy." He shot a glance at Hannibal, a gleam lighting his eyes.

Hannibal raised his eyebrows at his brother. How long

had he kept this bit of information to himself? Hasdrubal was trustworthy when the gates of Carthage were in question, but he relished the opportunity to withhold petty information just to have the upper hand.

"We are honored," Hannibal said. He disguised his frustration, noting Hasdrubal's smirk. He watched Massinissa struggle not to grin at his happiness with their approval. Hannibal was indeed pleased that Massinissa would join their family. Their mother had done well to secure an alliance with the Numidian King.

Massinissa shifted his weight from one foot to the other. "I'll leave you to your thoughts," he said. He left, with his shoulders back and his head high, every bit the regal king he'd been bred to be.

Both brothers watched him go.

Hannibal turned to his brother, who grinned expectantly. He wanted Hannibal to remark on him not sharing their mother's news.

Instead, Hannibal ignored the annoyance and brought up the more pressing subject he needed to discuss with Hasdrubal. "If the army goes into Italy, Carthage will be left unprotected," he said.

The joke died in Hasdrubal's face when he realized that his prank had fallen on preoccupied ears. "It would be difficult to pressure Rome if your flank wasn't covered," he said, regaining his stature and slipping back into the grim present.

"The Roman navy could easily out-maneuver us," Hannibal said.

"Leave a garrison behind here in Iberia," Hasdrubal said. "That would protect your retreat and be close enough to respond to any threat made on Carthage herself."

"I do not have many men to spare. The commander I leave must know how to make the most of a small defending garrison," Hannibal said. His brother wasn't going to like his decision. He looked away over the Iberian plains, where the grasses swayed like waves around the city walls.

"That is a difficult duty. No senior captain would appreciate being left behind," Hasdrubal said.

Hannibal turned to look Hasdrubal in the face. Until this moment, they were two brothers conversing. "You will stay behind here in Iberia with whatever men I can spare. Fortify Cartagena and be at the ready to sprint back to Carthage if duty necessitates."

Hasdrubal recoiled as if stung by a scorpion. Anger spilled over his face and across his brow. "You would leave me, your own brother, behind to languish as a coward?" Shock made his words ring louder than volume could have.

"You are no coward. There is nothing to prove." It was true. Hasdrubal had proved himself a brave soldier and a commander, but this was bigger than personal fame and glory.

Hasdrubal protested. "We are Barcas! We do not protect the flank. We are the spear's tip plunging into the hearts of our enemies." He took a breath, about to dive into a dramatic soliloquy.

"That is an order, Commander," Hannibal said.

Hasdrubal's face turned to a sneer. "In the hour of war, the great Hannibal is sure to keep all of the glory for himself."

Hannibal backhanded his brother across the face. It wasn't a vicious smack, but enough to force him backward half a step and break down his pride. "I am not asking you as a brother. I am asking you as a general to a subordinate. Do not test me, Hasdrubal."

A fire burned in Hasdrubal's eye. He reached down and put his hand on the hilt of his sword. He unsheathed it, raising its point to Hannibal.

Hannibal took a step toward Hasdrubal, looking him in the eye, daring him to strike. "Swing your blade, soldier."

Hasdrubal shuffled, his sword pointed at Hannibal's breastplate. Before Hasdrubal could move his sword, he gasped and stood perfectly still.

Hannibal focused his gaze behind Hasdrubal where Maherabal stood, the cold iron point of his weapon tickling the hairs on the back of the younger brother's neck. The Sacred Band was never far away. He didn't believe his brother would have run him through, but he was grateful to Maherabal for saving Hasdrubal from the embarrassment of backing down.

Hasdrubal dropped his sword and scampered away, disappearing from the city's wall.

Hannibal glanced at Maherabal who stood looking at him, waiting for an order. "Mobilize the men. We march at dawn."

CHAPTER 20

Mediterranean Coast

At daybreak, Hannibal sat on his horse near the sea front. He watched a flat-bottom skiff containing Sophonisba and Hamilcar begin its trek back to Carthage. Sophonisba held Hamilcar between her arms as he innocently waved goodbye to his father. Sophonisba's dark, sad eyes lock onto Hannibal. She tried to change his mind several times last night. He stifled a smile as he remembered the feel of her body pressing against his and her insistent kisses. She knew she couldn't change his mind, but she tried anyway. He loved her for it.

Hannibal watched them drift away, his face reflecting the sadness in Sophonisba's. He refused to blink, lest his emotions get away from him.

When his family was out of sight, he turned his horse around. As he galloped to the head of his mobilizing troops, he was no longer a husband and a father saying goodbye, possibly for the last time; he was a war general, determined to save the great city of Carthage from Rome.

He was a Barca.

CHAPTER 21

218 BCE, At the foot of the Pyrenees

For more than a week, Hannibal rode ahead of his sixty-thousand man army. To the left, rugged green hills rose and fell in the distance. To the right, he caught glimpses of the Iberian shoreline that guided them toward the mountains. Finally, the ground began to ascend beneath their feet, and the Pyrenees rose high in the distance, masked in whiteness and jutting into the sky like spear points.

Hannibal turned to the Iberian scout who rode beside him. "Is that a giant cloud over the mountain range?" he asked.

"No, sir," the scout said. "It's snow and ice." The man was short but broad, with a square forehead that gave way to bushy eyebrows and a bulbous nose. His face was chapped and hard from a life outdoors.

"Ice?" Hannibal asked. He searched his mind. The scout had described it before they'd left Cartagena in painful detail. The man was so serious, Hannibal couldn't help but toy with him a bit.

"Frozen water," the guide said. His brows drew down closer to his eyes. "Cold, hard, slippery to stand on? The most treacherous part of this journey? Sir?"

So this was ice. "Mountains full of frozen water," he murmured. "You could have mentioned this earlier."

An elephant trumpeted behind them. The scout looked behind him. "Don't tell me you didn't listen to my warnings about—I told you. I described—"

Hannibal turned a piercing look on the scout, who stopped speaking and looked away.

Did the scout really not know he was joking?

In truth, he had listened carefully to everything the scout had said, knowing it wasn't going to be easy moving sixty thousand troops, thirty war elephants, and all of their supplies over the mountains and into the Italian peninsula undetected.

Until he saw the mountains in front of him, he believed that elephants were big. Now he wasn't so sure.

CHAPTER 22

Three days later in the Pyrenees

The wind sprayed sideways sheets of icy snow at Hannibal's face as he led his horse forward, one painful step after another, up the incline. Snow slammed against the rock wall to his left, creating a wind tunnel that made stepping forward on the ice even more treacherous. To the right of the narrow path, the mountain plunged deep into a gorge filled with large, jagged rocks that promised death on impact.

Maherabal followed closely beside Hannibal. He was all that separated Hannibal from the edge of the mountain path, but if Hannibal slipped, he knew that Maherabal would not be able to stop his fall. They would go over together.

Maherabal stumbled and fell forward. He clawed at the ground and pushed himself upright. "Damn this snow to hell!" he said. "This is a godless place. Baal will never hear us from this miserable set of rocks."

"The men will hear you," Hannibal said.

Maherabal growled. "They'll hear a lot more than that when I slip off this ledge and impale myself on those rocks down there."

"Another complaint and I might push you myself," Hannibal said.

Maherabal didn't respond.

They trudged forward in silence.

"How are the elephants?" Hannibal asked. He knew he wasn't going to like the answer. The elephants were so big, and their feet so smooth on the bottom that they had an even harder time staying upright on the ice than his men did. The mahouts, who rode atop and directed them, were powerless when the massive creatures started to slip.

"Starved and cold," Maherabal said. "We seem to be losing one over the edge every few hours. Their flat feet slide right off the ice."

Hannibal saw a rock outcropping to his left and climbed it to see better. Looking out behind him, the line of men and beasts trailed down and disappeared into the falling snow until all he saw were smudges in the white.

Maherabal grunted as he pulled himself up beside Hannibal.

"We're maybe a quarter of the way in," Hannibal said.

"Food rations are running dangerously low, and there's no water left," Maherabal said.

"When we stop, show the men how to melt ice into water."

"Poor spirits prevail," Maherabal said, nodding.

"Only a fool could have high spirits in these mountains."

A short ways away, an elephant lost its footing and trumpeted while it struggled and then fell onto the trail, legs splayed. As it twisted against gravity, it crushed a dozen men underneath and threw the mahout from his perch. The men's screams barely carried over the roar of the wind.

Hannibal was a man of action, but he felt helpless. He

watched the elephant toss its giant head backward in an attempt to stand, but the momentum thrust the elephant backward and into the elephant behind it. The second elephant dropped to its knees, shrieking in terror as it crushed another dozen men and pushed another ten over the ledge and into the rocky abyss below. The mahout toppled over, but instead of falling to the ground, the restraining rope twisted around him, and he hung head-down, dangling in midair.

The first elephant slid down the path, angling closer and closer to the edge. The second struggled against the ice for another second before it stumbled over the edge. In the next instant, the first elephant went over, dragging over twenty men with it and leaving several more facedown in the path, to be tripped over by the line of soldiers marching behind them.

Hannibal heard the crunch of bones, and the mountain seemed to groan and shudder as the weight fell from its shoulders. A hundred feet below, blood spattered against the jagged rocks and froze, turning the snow into a scattered pink.

Everything but the wind stood still for a moment.

"Men!" Hannibal shouted. "Forward to Rome!"

At his command, the frozen men tore their gazes from the sight below and pushed forward, willing themselves to put one foot in front of the other.

CHAPTER 23

In the Pyrenees

As suddenly as it came, the storm left, but the cold remained. The air was so frigid that it hurt Hannibal's lungs to inhale deeply, and he could see his breath pillow in white clouds as he exhaled. *Curse this cold!* he thought. It was no less dangerous than the storm had been. Countless of his men had grown delirious from the cold. One instant they shivered and the next they were burning up. Some took off their clothing to lie down in the snow, closed their eyes, and never woke up.

They were nearing the top of the mountain now, almost to the Italian side. The higher they marched, the more difficult it became to breathe, and now their footsteps were labored and accompanied by animal grunts.

No trees grew this high, and as Hannibal looked around, he saw whitewashed vistas and blue ridges that gleamed in the cold sun. The mountain range stretched as far as he could see in all directions. In the valleys between ridges, patches of trees somehow stayed green and alive in this godforsaken wasteland. It was breathtaking. It was also life-taking. But he had made it this far. The beauty around him was the sole reward for surviving. Was this a sign of what was to come?

Thousands lost for nothing but a view? He prayed not.

"General! Sir!" someone shouted.

Hannibal turned to see four members of the Sacred Band appear ahead of the army on the trail. They dragged a bound man behind them.

"General, we've found a spy," the guard said.

"Unbind him," Hannibal said. He motioned for the troops to halt behind him and watched the guards untie the man.

The imposter appeared to be a scout. His face was mostly hidden by a scruffy beard, and his clothing looked impenetrable.

"What is your business here?" Hannibal asked.

Hannibal was surprised to hear the scout speak in accented Carthaginian: "These mountains are our home, and we have every right to know who passes."

"Hannibal Barca and his army from Africa and Iberia," Hannibal said.

"You haven't paid the toll or made arrangements with the tribes here," the scout said.

"We were not aware of a toll." Hannibal turned to Maherabal, who stood to his right. "Get my scout."

Maherabal slipped away, down the line of troops to find the Iberian Scout.

Hannibal turned his attention back to the scout in front of him. "Is that what your people wish for? A tribute in exchange for safe passage?"

"That's all," the scout said. He met Hannibal's eye deliberately.

Hannibal didn't blink. He had nothing to offer the scout and his tribe even if he had been inclined to do so. "I am not a man to pay tribute or demand safe passage," he said. "I dare you to stop me from descending into Italy."

The scout's eye glinted. "You seem like a reasonable man, but let me warn you *General*, that making war on a Celt in his homeland is a dangerous mistake."

Hannibal smiled and took a step closer to the scout. This man had his grudging respect. He wouldn't kill him unless he had to. It had been his father's policy not to slay an honorable man if he could help it. He slapped the scout on the shoulder. "You're not afraid. I like that."

Maherabal returned with the Iberian scout and half a dozen other captured Celtic scouts.

"The only war I seek is against Rome," Hannibal said. He pointed to the Iberian scout and gestured to the Celt in front of him. "Walk with this Celt. Find out the best passageways and secret to draining food from this godforsaken place."

"How do I know if he's lying to me?" the Iberian protested.

Hannibal looked at the Celt as he spoke. "Because he knows what we'll do if he does."

The Celt may have gulped at that, but Hannibal couldn't tell under the massive black beard.

He turned to Maherabal and motioned to the other six Celt prisoners. "Kill them," he said.

Maherabal immediately drew his sword and lopped off the head of the closest Celt. The other members of the Sacred Band did the same. The decapitated Celts crumpled to the ground, and their bloody heads rolled over the snow.

Maherabal crouched and grabbed a dead man's leg by the ankle. "Food is scarce," he said, looking at Hannibal.

The idea of eating human flesh repulsed him, but before

he could respond, Massinissa stepped forward from where he had watched the scene near the halted troops.

"Absolutely not," Massinissa said, narrowing his eyes at Maherabal. "We will die before becoming barbarians." The two men stared each other down.

Hannibal looked at Massinissa and nodded. "Push them over," he said.

The Sacred Band pushed the bodies over the edge of the mountain. They freefell for a second and crashed into the icy rocks far below them, rolling off in trails of red spatter.

The remaining Celt watched his former comrades tumble with barely contained horror. The beard was no longer fearless.

Hannibal motioned for the march to continue.

The Iberian scout gave the Celt a swift kick, and the two fell in line with the troops as they continued their ascent.

CHAPTER 24

In the Pyrenees

The wind at the top was strong enough to cut through every layer of clothing Hannibal wore and almost slashed apart his will to take another step. Every step felt simultaneously hopeless and odds-defying. He doubled over in a fruitless attempt to duck the cold and even out the heaviness of his armor. Snow flurries swirled through the air and hit him like a hundred icy needles at once.

"Father," he whispered. The word froze in his beard. What would his father tell him now?

The words imprinted themselves on his mind: "Lion of Carthage!" They strengthened him, and he took one more step.

Behind him, his men traipsed on, keeping as close together as they could and rotating positions against the wind to preserve energy.

The Iberian scout returned to Hannibal from the trail up ahead. "There's a clearing just over this ridge," he said. "Then begins the descent."

"Fine. Have the men make camp there, and rest for the climb down," Hannibal said.

The scout hesitated. "Sir, I think you should have a look first."

Hannibal and Maherabal pushed forward, following the scout over the steep embankment. The scout gestured to a clearing a little ways below them. Rather than a rocky white expanse, the clearing was filled with thousands of waiting Celtic warriors. Blue dye covered their faces, and their shields formed an impenetrable wall.

Hannibal knew that his men, exhausted and malnourished, were all but defeated by the mountain. They were no match for the giant Celts, not now. Even the Romans feared the Celts, and the Romans weren't afraid of anyone. His only option was to persuade the Celts to peace. His gut told him that his Celtic prisoner was someone important, which he could use to his advantage. The six he'd killed didn't matter. They'd shown no honor.

"Barbarians," Maherabal muttered.

"Yes," Hannibal said, "and we're on their mountain."

"Stop the march?" Maherabal asked.

"Yes. And bring me our Celt. I want to talk with the Chieftain, man-to-man."

"Sir, are you sure that's wise? I hear the Celts would sooner cut off a foreigner's arms and legs and leave him to die a slow, painful death than let him beg."

"This is no land for beggars," Hannibal said. "The Chieftain wants respect, a reason for safe passage. I can offer him one."

"Our Celt?"

Hannibal nodded. He climbed down from the ridge and mounted his horse.

Maherabal brought the Celtic scout forward on a tired horse. It was one of the healthiest animals they had, Hannibal thought grimly. He knew he was chancing everything on the hope that this Celt was someone important to the Chieftain.

They picked their way over the ridge and descended into the plain in front of the Celtic army. The scout kept pace beside him, and recognition lit his face for a moment.

Hannibal took hope from that and pulled his horse to a stop as the Chieftain stepped out of the phalanx to meet him.

"Is it African custom to kill strangers in a strange land?" the Chieftain asked. He stood nearly as tall as Hannibal's horse, and the long feathers in his peaked helmet only made him seem larger.

"I have come to kill Romans," he said. "Your scouts were spying. I had no reason not to believe that they worked for Rome."

"Yet this one lived?" the Chieftain said, cutting a glance at the scout next to Hannibal. A look passed between the two of them.

They know each other, Hannibal thought with relief. Was this scout the Chieftain's son? "This one had courage. He earned my respect," he said.

The Chieftain looked over his shoulder at his five thousand soldiers. "You may find it very difficult to pass."

"No army can stand between me and Rome."

"Bold words for an African whose army has met winter for the first time."

Hannibal knew the Chieftain was right. His men didn't know how to fight in snow. They were barely surviving. He had to avoid a battle. "Your scout tells me that you are no friend of Rome," he said, carefully enunciating each syllable.

The Chieftain raised his eyebrows and glanced over at the scout. "Is that what my scout told you?"

The scout lowered his head.

The Chieftain's eyes returned to Hannibal. "What's in it for me?"

It was time to take a risk. "Your son. Uninjured."

Maherabal's knife was in his hand in a flash, poised to strike the young scout's sword hand from his wrist.

"Do you threaten me?" The Chieftain's glare turned dangerous. His hand went to his hilt.

Not blinking, Hannibal continued. "If you'd rather kill Romans than strangers, consider this a small incentive."

The Chieftain unsheathed his sword faster than Baal with a bolt of lightning, stopping his blade a hair width from Hannibal's throat. "I can find my own incentives."

Hannibal took shallow breaths and felt his mind narrowing its focus. "Join with Africa against Rome. Together, we can't fail."

The Chieftain's impenetrable eyes lightened, but he didn't drop his sword. "What promise do I have that once Rome is vanquished, you will not become the new Rome?" the Chieftain asked.

"I have no heart for empire," Hannibal said. "One man's domination over another is unjust and dishonorable in the eyes of the gods. Carthage leads an alliance of kingdoms. Each is allowed to agree or disagree with Carthage's decisions. Carthage has no interest in ruling them. Our alliance is based on honor and respect. The same honor I recognized in your scout."

There was a long pause while the Chieftain considered this. Slowly, he lowered his sword from Hannibal's throat and looked over at the scout. "Come here, boy," he said to the scout.

The scout glanced at Hannibal and hesitated.

Maherabal put his knife away.

"This is my son, Kelin," the Chieftain said. "You spared his life. We will lead you safely down into Lombardy. Our scouts will feed Rome lies so that your arrival there will go undetected."

"Thank you, friend," Hannibal said. He took off his glove and offered the Chieftain his hand to shake. "Hannibal Barca."

The Chieftain firmly grabbed his hand. "Minerix," he said.

"Minerix," Hannibal repeated the Chieftain's name.

Kelin dismounted and stood next to his father.

CHAPTER 25

Present Day Northern Italy

With the Celtic army guiding their descent, it took only a few days to reach the grassy lakes district in Northern Italy. Hannibal was relieved to be rid of the snow and breathe without the air stabbing his lungs. His men looked beaten half to death, and half of his war elephants had perished. After the journey they'd had, Hannibal was surprised they hadn't lost them all.

Green hills spread out around them, with terraced farms and a distant village cut into the hillsides. The sun slanted toward the western horizon, casting the valleys in shadows and making them look deeper than they were.

Minerix led them around a lake with waves that sparkled orange in the glowing sunset.

Hannibal's stomach growled. It was past time for a meal, but Minerix insisted they press on until they reached the village.

It was nearly dark by the time they arrived. The armies stopped at the edge of the village to set up camp and wait.

"We must tell the people of this village that we wish them to join us," Hannibal said. "We are only here to kill Roman soldiers."

"These villagers are aware of your needs," Minerix said. "They've pooled together to provide a few days of hot meals for your men."

"Their generosity will be remembered when Roman gold is spilled," Hannibal said. His eyes scanned gentle hills sloping gently up on all sides; the valley made him feel exposed.

"Now that you're in Italy, I cannot stop Roman eyes from seeing you," Minerix said. "You must move quickly to retain the element of surprise."

Hannibal nodded, understanding how little time they had.

Maherabal galloped over to them and dismounted in one smooth motion. "We have thirty-five thousand men and seventeen elephants."

"Cavalry?" Hannibal asked.

"Eight thousand still with mounts."

Hannibal nodded, doing some quick figuring in his head. "That will be enough," he said. "Now we're racing the Roman spies."

CHAPTER 26

Senate Chamber, Rome

The Roman Senate Chamber was a white marble room with plain white columns running down one side. The whiteness of the room was only broken by the purple stripes that fell from the senators' shoulders. The senators stood around Maximus, who had the floor. The consul, Sempronius, sat in a chair behind him.

Scipio watched from the back of the group, his new white robe itching the back of his neck. He missed his armor right now. Being the youngest member of the council had seemed like a dream come true, but from where he stood at the back of the room, it couldn't be clearer that his youth was not doing him any favors. These men were old and proud. Listening to a young man was beneath them.

"Like a thief, Hannibal stole over the mountains," Maximus said. His words came out as angry barks. "He has been confirmed with forty thousand men in Lombardy."

"How did he manage to sneak past Minerix?" one of the senators asked.

"The Celts led his army down from the mountains," Maximus said.

"That can't be true," the senator said. "We paid them for their loyalty. They took our payment."

"Apparently they expected more," another senator said.

"What did I tell you?" another senator chimed in. "Barbarians don't understand loyalty. I told you it was naive to think otherwise."

Mumbles spread through the room.

Maximus rose, his hand in the air. He wasn't the most powerful man in the room, but he had the most charisma.

The room fell silent.

"How many of our legions are battle-ready?" someone asked.

"We can send four now and leave two to protect Rome," Maximus said. "I propose a counter strike immediately. The longer we allow those Carthaginians to walk on our roads, the more comfortable they'll get here, and the more trouble they will cause."

Sempronius stood from the chair behind Maximus as if from a throne. "An immediate attack," he exclaimed. "Rome will not stand for other armies on her soil. The mere thought sickens me."

The senators clapped and cheered. One of them did a war call.

Scipio shifted his weight and remained silent. He felt certain that an immediate attack was what Hannibal was counting on. "He's mimicking Alexander," he said, speaking loudly to be heard over the applause.

The chamber grew quiet. The other senators stared at him, surprised that he had spoken. Maximus and Sempronius looked at him with disgust. Scipio knew that there was an unspoken rule that he was to keep his mouth shut, and they were insulted that he had broken it. Still, he wasn't a kid who didn't know anything; he'd studied all of the great military tacticians.

"Young Scipio?" Maximus said. "It is rare that such an inexperienced voice is heard on matters of war."

Ignoring the comment and Maximus's satisfied smirk, Scipio continued. "Hannibal is mimicking Alexander the Great, and he's counting on us to rush to meet him in battle. In our haste, he will gain the strategic advantage."

Sempronius clapped, but the look on his face was mocking.

Scipio refused to look away from the consul's contemptuous smile. He was right, and he knew it. Sempronius and Maximus were fools not to hear his words because of their own prejudices.

"Ah, young Scipio," Sempronius said, "I see that you are living up to the brash example of your namesake."

The senators chuckled.

Scipio's face went hot, but he didn't blink. "He's luring us to him. We'll tire our legions crossing the Tiber and then he will launch his attack."

Sempronius's chuckle turned serious. "I'd suggest you leave the tactics to those who have been to battle before. How many campaigns have you led?"

The room rang with unpleasant laughter.

Scipio felt his face grow hotter, but he didn't look away. His father had gone up against Hamilcar in the first war and had taught Scipio everything he knew. Even if he had never led a battle, he knew that his judgment was sound.

"What if they have elephants?" Scipio asked, remembering the Battle of Heraclea. The Romans might have won against King Pyrrhus had it not been for the surprise elephant attack.

Maximus laughed. "You think they brought elephants over the mountains? Men can barely travel through the Alps, no less elephants."

"And yet Hannibal is here," Scipio said.

"Yes, and the longer we wait to act, the more time they have to rest up and buy up more of Rome's allies," Maximus said. "Ready four legions at once. They march at daybreak."

And with those words, everyone forgot about Scipio and his opinions.

CHAPTER 27

Council Room, Carthage

Lady Barca looked away from Ida Hanna's passionate speech-making at the front of the council room. A few people subtly nodded at his words. A few others glared. Most looked caught somewhere between.

Sapanibal shifted in her seat. She had begged not to come today, but Lady Barca had insisted. Sapanibal needed to learn how to hold her own at council, and to do that she needed to begin learning how Carthaginian politics worked and how quickly someone like Ida Hanna could change the fate of Carthage with his jealousy and impatience.

"In patriotic fervor we raised a sixty-thousand man army, and what does Hannibal do with them? He marches them over the two most dangerous mountain passes known to man and gods alike. Reports indicate that half of those men are dead now. It's murder!" Ida said, slamming his hands on the tabletop in punctuation.

A few people applauded.

Lady Barca slowly stood. Her blood boiled, but her face and her voice were placid. "It's not murder, Ida. It's war," she said, speaking in the tone she usually reserved for the neighbors' unruly children. "It's an art form that you are not accustomed to."

There were a few murmurs of agreement. Ida's eyes narrowed at Lady Barca and he looked away. "One need not be a battle-hardened veteran to recognize the sub-par leadership of Carthage's standing army," he sneered. "Carthage has blindly trusted the Barcas with our warriors for too long. I move that we vote to relieve Hannibal of his command."

Lady Barca was surprised by the number of cheers echoing off of the council room walls. Had these men no loyalty to their own country? Her son was fighting a war to preserve Carthage from Rome's sneaky attacks on their resources, and they treated it as if he had gone on some frivolous campaign simply because he felt like it. Hannibal was far too wise to sacrifice his country just because of a personal vendetta against Rome.

"My husband, Hamilcar, is regarded as one of Carthage's greatest generals, but without so much as one battle, my son has already moved an army closer to Rome than Hamilcar ever dreamed," Lady Barca said.

"At what cost?" Ida said. His narrowed eyes would have shot invisible daggers at her if they could.

"Hannibal does not need our criticism and doubt," she said. "He needs reinforcements. Let us call on our Greek allies to transport another twenty thousand warriors to the shores of Italy."

"You Barcas are insatiable," Ida said. "You dominate this city and are willing to sacrifice Carthage's finest blood in order to do so. I say enough!"

The room grew silent as Geromachus, an elder of the council and the most widely respected man in Carthage, stood on shaking legs. He voice faltered, and the words came slowly as he spoke. "It is true that we have long trusted the Barcas in the arena of war, and Hannibal has yet to fall short of his ancestors. Let him fight with those who would march with him, and we will keep the rest of Carthage's men at home in case his plan fails." Geromachus nodded his head with finality and lowered himself slowly back to his seat.

Many in the chamber nodded in agreement.

Lady Barca pursed her lips. It was a clever compromise, but she feared that it wouldn't be enough. If reports of Hannibal's casualties while crossing the mountains could be trusted, then he was down too many men to take Rome. But if she pressed the issue any further, she'd be down too many men in Carthage.

CHAPTER 28

Trebia River

Fog hovered over the Trebia River, casting the water's surface with a murky gray. It wasn't a large river. No one would get ambushed in a river like this.

The fleeting reminder of his father brought him strength as he looked out on the flat ground that lay between the Carthaginian camp and the river. Massinissa and Maherabal stood on either side of him.

"My scouts say that the Roman force is a half-day's journey down the river," Massinissa said. "Four legions by their count. They'll outnumber us by twenty thousand men."

"Perfect," Hannibal said.

Maherabal nodded, but Massinissa raised his eyebrows.

"Perfect?" Massinissa asked.

"Should we cross the river before they arrive?" Maherabal asked.

"No," Hannibal said. "Form ranks on this side of the river and wait. They'll be anxious for battle. Let them cross." Having to cross the river first would tire them out some and give the Carthaginian forces the upper hand. He'd read about the strategy as a young boy, learning the tactics of Alexander the

Great. This was the perfect time to use it.

"And the horses?" Massinissa asked.

Hannibal pointed down to a hidden ravine just upstream from the Romans' approach. "Hide the cavalry there. When the last Roman has set foot on our side of the river, charge their right flank."

Massinissa nodded. "Yes, sir."

"And the elephants?" Maherabal asked.

"Divide them into two groups. They'll enter from the right and left flanks."

Maherabal nodded.

Silence stretched between them. Hannibal smelled the dampness of the riverbank and heard a metallic clicking sound somewhere in the distance. The Romans were coming, but a calm stole over him. He had prayed to Anath, goddess of love and war, and could feel her blessing firmly upon him. He curved his fingers around the hilt of his sword, tracing the hilt's cold, gentle curve with his thumb.

CHAPTER 29

Trebia River

The fog had dissipated by the time the Roman flat boats reached the battle site. They disembarked opposite the Carthaginian camp and began to erect fortifications. Hannibal watched in consternation. They weren't as eager for battle as he'd expected. His entire strategy depended on the Romans carelessly rushing into battle. If they weren't in disarray, then he needed a new strategy. He paced a few steps closer, noting the curve of some of the helmets. Were the Romans employing Celtic mercenaries?

Hannibal felt the shifting of his army behind him as they watched the Roman camps and waited for Hannibal's command. His soldiers were professionals, not volunteers like the Romans. He felt confident that their experience would make up for their lack of numbers as long as he could come up with a better strategy. Many of them had fought against Rome with General Hamilcar during the first war, and today's skirmish didn't daunt them.

Hannibal trotted up and down the front line until an idea came to him. He found Minerix and approached him.

"I see Celtic auxiliaries in the Roman ranks," Hannibal

said.

"I would expect so," Minerix said. "Most Celts in this area are loyal to Rome."

"Would you be able to get a message to the Celtic Chieftain across the river?"

Minerix frowned for a moment, letting the meaning of Hannibal's question sink in. He nodded slowly. "Line up my men in front of the auxiliaries," he said.

"Good man, Minerix," Hannibal said. He finished his trot down the front line and then returned to the middle.

From his place at the lead, he shouted so that all of his men could hear. "Today we begin our Italian campaign. You are all soldiers. You have tasted blood before. Across the River Trebia stand sixty thousand boys without hair on their chins. On this day, let Rome remember what Carthage thinks of the red empire. What we think of oath breakers."

His men didn't cheer like children at the arena; they stood straighter, tightened their hands on their weapons, and snarled like lions. A new intensity rose from the ranks. They drew their swords and clanked them loudly against their shields, stone-faced and ready for battle.

Hannibal turned his horse to face the river. The Romans were still setting up camp. He would have to fix that before they got too comfortable. He drew his sword and yelled, "Iberian archers to distance!"

The two hundred Iberian archers wove through the front lines and jogged toward the river, stopping within striking distance of the Roman camp. Their bows were taller than their bodies, but they handled them as if they were extensions of their hands. They strung arrows swiftly and lay down on their backs to draw the bows back with their feet. They lay still, waiting for Hannibal's command.

Maherabal rode up. "Massinissa is in place."

Hannibal nodded. The pre-battle restlessness left him, and calmness embraced him. The strategy had been set, and it would work. He smiled. "Send him my greetings," he said. Then he raised his voice so that the archers could hear him. "Loose at will!"

The bows thumped as they decompressed. Arrows blanketed the battlefield in fleeting shade as the wooden missiles shot forward, crossed the river, and bit into the unfortified Roman camp.

CHAPTER 30

Trebia River

Scipio saw the wall of arrows soaring through the camp before anyone else. "Fall in!" he yelled. "Fall in! Shields up! Order and discipline will win the day!"

A few men around him were struck by arrows in their backs and sides. Their anguished cries echoed through the camp as they fell to the ground. Their breastplates were no match for the strength of the Carthaginian arrows, which cut through the armor like knives through bread. The rest of the soldiers scrambled to form ranks and organize their shields in the Roman tortoiseshell formation.

"We've got them!" Scipio yelled. "Fall in!"

A young soldier, encouraged by Scipio's words, pulled himself to his feet, jerked an arrow out of his leg, and fell into rank with his shield out in front.

Another wave of arrows flew in their direction, piercing through the shields. An arrow slid through the shield and helmet of the man to Scipio's left, and the man dropped dead instantly. Scipio kicked the man's body out of the way. The soldiers behind him hesitated, not wanting to meet the fallen soldier's fate. Scipio jerked a man forward.

"Fall in!" he yelled at the terrified young man. "Order and discipline."

CHAPTER 31

Trebia River

Behind the Roman ranks, Maximus stood with the consul, Sempronius, watching the onslaught of Carthaginian arrows pummel his ranks. The Consular Guard surrounded the two of them, at the ready, but their swords were defenseless against the arrows.

Maximus's mind raced, and he was frozen to the spot. "Their archers outdistance ours by forty paces. We'd have to be mid-river to hit their formations."

Sempronius frowned. "Well, they can't win the battle with arrows alone."

The two watched in silence for a moment. Screams lit the air as more Romans fell. They had to do something.

"Hannibal has left space on the field. We'll need to cross the river to gain an offensive position," Sempronius said.

"Yes," Maximus said. "Offensive position. That is certainly more desirable." He shook his head, trying to clear his mind and think through a workable strategy, but his breaths came in shallower gasps.

"More desirable than waiting for hours while his archers thin our ranks," Sempronius said.

Neither of them moved, and Maximus realized with renewed fear that neither of them wanted to give the call to march against the Great Hannibal Barca. It had been one thing to stare down Hannibal's mother; it was quite another to face the man himself.

He took a deep break and kicked his horse forward. "Form ranks!" he yelled, hating that his voice warbled. He cleared his throat and tried again. "Form ranks to cross the river!"

Men fell in line, casting furtive glances at the archers and the men falling in front of them.

"Confidence, men!" Maximus shouting, hoping he sounded far more confident than he felt. It had been many years since he'd led a battle.

CHAPTER 32

Trebia River

Hannibal heard the command to cross the river. This was it. He had forced them to action, and now it was time for the real battle to start. He ran a hand over the scar along his eye, wiping away a lone bead of sweat before it dropped into his eye. The Romans would cross the Trebia, and his men were lined up waiting. Despite their inferior numbers, they couldn't lose. Baal must be smiling on Carthage.

He sat atop his horse, calmly watching the Roman legions move forward into the river. They kept their shields in formation as much as they could in the elbow deep water.

He held his arm up, signaling for his soldiers' attention, prepping for his command to charge. He surveyed his ranks. The Celts lined up to the right and left, mirroring the Celts in the Romans' formation. The middle formation was a mix of Carthaginian natives, Libyans, and Iberians. The cavalry was a mix of Carthaginians and Numidians, hidden in their ravine, tensed and ready to attack.

Minerix trotted by holding a tribal horn. He held it to his lips and blew. Short, guttural blasts issued forth in choppy succession. Moments later, the same pattern repeated from across the field by the Roman Celts. Minerix responded with several short blasts.

Maherabal rode forward, drawing Hannibal's attention. "Now?" he called.

"Hold! Wait for my command," Hannibal called back. He returned his gaze to the Roman ranks crossing the river. If he didn't wait for enough of the army to cross, he risked forcing them to a hasty retreat that would allow a reformation and renewed attack.

The closer they got, the more focused he became. The moment the Roman army hit the point of no return, Hannibal pointed his sword toward the river. Spurring his horse, he yelled, "Carthage! Charge!"

Without a moment's hesitation, Hannibal's forces fell behind him as he led the charge at a breakneck pace. The thunder of footsteps roared around him, gaining momentum.

The Romans struggled to form ranks as they pulled themselves out of the river. Their boots were wet, and the riverbank grew soggier with each wet footfall that trod on it.

Hannibal saw Maximus and Sempronius crossing the river on a flat boat rather than wading through at the front of their men.

"Cavalry engage!" Sempronius yelled as he urged his horse from the boat to the sloppy bank.

Maximus followed him yelling, "Form ranks and push to dry land!" His shrill voice betrayed his panic.

Hannibal nodded. This would work. He looked over his shoulder and called back, "Elephants, forward charge!"

A second before the Carthaginian front lines crashed against the Romans, the elephants emerged from the forests on either side of the field and barreled ahead with deafening force.

Hannibal, leading the front lines, watched the Roman soldiers' eyes go wide with terror at the sight of the twenty-foot beasts bearing down on them.

This was destined to be a short battle.

CHAPTER 33

Trebia River

The Romans drew back in terror. With no command coming from Maximus or Sempronius behind them to keep them on course, the men shied away. The beasts had wrinkled gray skin and giant tusks larger than any man's sword. Their noses extended to the ground and swung back and forth. They capsized men with little effort, clipping off the edges of the half-formed tortoise shell formation and sending men flying.

"Hold rank!" Scipio shouted. "Slay the beasts!" His words had little impact. The fear in their eyes turned to panic, and many of them ran back toward the river, sending whole sections of the shielded phalanx into disarray.

"Hold rank!" Scipio shouted again. "Hold! Slay the beasts when they get here! Slay the beasts!"

The men regained their courage and set their heels just in time to meet the Carthaginian forces. They pressed their shields together leaving only enough room for their spears between.

Scipio continued to shout at the top of his lungs, anything to keep his men fighting. A retreat now would mean certain defeat. The Carthaginians wouldn't hesitate to pursue them

into the river. But at least Rome had the advantage of numbers.

Catching Scipio's eye was the great General Hannibal. After looking Scipio down, Hannibal clashed with two Romans
at once, penetrating their shields with his sword and slicing
their heads off in two fluid strikes.

CHAPTER 34

Trebia River

The Sacred Band surrounded Hannibal as he turned his horse in a circle, looking for the weakest links in the Roman front line. He brought his horse back a few steps and kicked the steed forward, urging it to leap over the wall of shields. The hooves hit the formation, and several men fell under the weight of the horse. The horse struggled for a moment to regain its footing while Hannibal sliced the helmets clean off of the necks of the Romans surrounding him on all sides.

The Sacred Band followed him, slicing off the arms of any Roman who dared point his weapon in Hannibal's direction.

Maherabal turned backward on his horse. Kneeling and balancing on the strength of his ankles, he swung his sword with one hand and pulled knives hidden in his armor with the other, which he threw at the Romans who tried to surround them. His face was deadly, determined, and covered with the blood of the enemy.

Another member of the Sacred Band leaned off his horse, ducking Roman swords, collecting Maherabal's daggers from the heap of Roman corpses before plunging them into the skulls of the Romans who moved in to replace their dead comrades.

Hannibal moved at the front of the Band, blowing through the Roman ranks and cutting down Romans with calculated precision. A power outside of his own strength seemed to have overtaken him, for he was possessed with manic fury. He slashed his way into the Roman ranks with his only goal to take out as many Romans as possible.

Screams surrounded them.

CHAPTER 35

Trebia River

At the right flank, Minerix led the Celts at full speed toward the Celts in the Roman line. His soldiers didn't slow as they approached the Roman line. Instead, the Celts on Rome's side turned to race with their Celtic brethren at the Roman legion in a united attack.

Scipio watched the sudden desertion of the Celtic mercenaries in horror. This was worse than he'd feared. With boiling blood, he slashed through anything in his way, turning to bloodlust to cushion the betrayal. If Maximus and Sempronius had taken him seriously, they might have avoided this twist in fate. But *no*, they thought he was a child.

He glanced behind him, noting that they were nowhere near the front lines. Who was a child now? The cowards!

"Left flank hold!" Scipio shouted. Yells split the air, as the Romans tried to call the Celts back to their line. The Celts didn't heed the calls, instead rapidly felling one surprised Roman after another.

Scipio swung his sword harder and faster, even while he began to see the futility of the effort. These soldiers weren't trained for this. They were young boys, volunteers who had been led to believe that this would be an easy battle, in and out with nothing but a few scratches. It would bolster their résumés and give them a leg up running for the Senate. Instead, they were being slaughtered, and all Scipio could do was keep yelling for them to hold their ranks and fight like the men they never were. Here he would die for the pride of a bunch of hopeful politicians. He let his rage fuel him. There was nothing left for any of them but this battle, and he refused to go like a coward.

CHAPTER 36

Trebia River

Maximus and Sempronius watched in horror as the Celts behind their lines turned on them and clashed against the Romans.

"Damn the Celts!" Maximus yelled. "Damn them to the River Styx!"

At that moment, the elephants crushed their way through the tumultuous Roman line, blasting trumpet sounds that enveloped the battlefield. Even their echoes were louder than the terror of soldiers meeting their end.

The Carthaginians expertly moved together to funnel the elephants into the heart of the fray. The mahouts on top steered them directly into the tortoise shell formation of the shields, crushing the formation, bringing more terror and pandemonium to the Roman ranks, and driving them back toward the river.

Sempronius urged his horse ahead several yards, yelling, "Hold the middle lines against the beasts! Slash their knees! Spear the men on top!"

But the men were too terrified of being walloped by a flailing trunk or gored by their tusks. All they could do was scream and swing their weapons uselessly as they were pushed back.

Maximus scanned the field. The right flanked had caved in and was pushed back to the river. The middle struggled to keep formation and was beginning to crumble. The left flank, led by Scipio, was the only flank that managed to keep a semblance of control. He glowered at the realization that if they won this battle, the credit would belong to Scipio.

CHAPTER 37

Trebia River

Hannibal stuck his bloody sword through a centurion's chest. The moment the Roman fell, the General paused to look around him. A soldier came at him from his right, and he dodged the tired sword, bringing his own weapon around at lightning speed and splitting the man in two.

It looked promising for Carthage. They were ready to launch the final attack. He spun his horse around. "Carthage for victory!" he shouted as he disappeared behind Carthaginian lines. One section of the Roman line still held the field, and his final strategy would break it.

He dismounted and grabbed a flaming arrow from a camp fire. He strung it through the longbow, lay down on the ground, and took careful aim. He inhaled. Releasing the bowstring with his breath, the arrow soared like a comet through the sky, arching toward the Romans' left flank.

"Now, Massinissa!" he shouted.

For a split second as he stood and unsheathed his sword, Hannibal left himself unprotected. As his flaming arrow climbed higher into the sky, a Roman sharpshooter spied his target and drove an arrow through Hannibal's thigh and into the ground beneath him.

He grunted. The force distracted him more than the pain. He struggled to sit up and take account of the damages.

Maherabal leaped to his side and three other members of the Guard surrounded him. They broke off the spearhead that stuck into the ground and cut off the shaft of the arrow that protruded from Hannibal's leg.

"Can you stand?" one of the guards asked. "We have to get you out of here."

Hannibal pushed the guards away once they helped him to his feet. He tested the leg. It held him. It would hurt later, but right now he felt nothing.

"This wound must be cleaned," one of the guards insisted, trying to usher him away from the battlefield toward the camp behind the Carthaginian lines.

Hannibal stood his ground. He met Maherabal's eyes, the only one of his guards who understood that he didn't plan to leave the battle before it was over. Hannibal jerked what was left of the arrow shaft from his leg, and stood upright, relieved that blood didn't start spurting. It hadn't hit a main artery.

He ripped a chunk of his tunic off, wrapped it tightly around the wound, and knotted it in place. He shrugged off the Guards and turned his attention back to the battle.

Massinissa's cavalry emerged from the ravine at the Romans' left flank and slammed into it with an energy that the Romans couldn't match. Victory was at hand.

Hannibal raised his sword and rushed back toward the front lines, yelling as he went. "To the river, men! Send them floating back to Rome!"

The Carthaginians surged ahead as if they had been saving energy for this very moment.

Within minutes, the Roman legions collapsed beyond repair. They were on the home stretch.

CHAPTER 38

Trebia River

Scipio sensed the moment Carthage had won the battle. The legions around him disintegrated and his soldiers sprinted for the river. Many leaped into the water in a mad attempt to swim for safety.

"Don't turn your backs!" Scipio shouted. "Fight like men!"

But it didn't matter what he shouted anymore. Whether they turned their backs and ran or stood and fought, death was imminent.

A member of the Roman cavalry reared his horse back and dashed toward the river.

Scipio grabbed the coward's cloak, jerking him from his mount. The horse ran away screaming. The soldier squirmed in the dirt, tears running down his face.

"You are an officer of the Roman legion!" Scipio yelled. "Without courage, your life is worthless!"

The officer pushed him away. "Preach to the dead men!" He kicked at Scipio's face. "Let me go!" He writhed until Scipio lost his grasp. The officer crawled away and dove into the river. A Carthaginian arrow caught him in the back as he swam, and the officer disappeared below the water, leaving a stream of red in his wake.

It served him right, Scipio thought. A coward deserved a coward's death. What was more disgraceful than an arrow in the back?

CHAPTER 39

Trebia River

Maximus watched the collapse of the Roman lines from his mount near the river, surrounded by six members of the consular guard. All around him, soldiers threw themselves into the water to escape death. Where had they gone wrong? They had a good twenty-thousand man advantage on the Carthaginian forces. They couldn't lose. He'd never suffered such a defeat before. It was shameful. He'd been so sure of success. Beat back the Carthaginians, deplete their resources to fight, cut off their trade routes, and take their city while it starved. It was such a simple plan. His ears rang, and he couldn't tell if it was from the battle cries and clanking of weapons around him, or if it was from the realization that it would be better to die here today than to return to Rome a failure.

He had declared war on Carthage believing with all of his heart that Carthage didn't have the resources or connections to put up a fight. He'd declared war believing that they would try to stop the war diplomatically. They'd give up Saguntum. They'd give up Cartagena. They'd give up fragments of their territories until they had nothing left to feed their city and nothing to offer their allies. That's how it should have gone. He hadn't expected this battle. Not like this.

He would never see Rome, his wife, his mistress, or the Senate Chamber again. The citizens would never let him wear the purple stripes again. His whole life dedicated to achieving the highest office in Rome…it wasn't fair that it would end like this.

Sempronius rode up to Maximus, the look on his face reflecting Maximus's feelings exactly.

"Four legions lost in one day," Maximus said. "We are disgraced men."

"We have to report back to the Senate and fortify Rome. Hannibal will not rest," Sempronius said.

In that instant, the Carthaginian front broke through the last remaining Romans and made straight for the consular guard. The guards fought back, but it was useless.

A perfectly aimed spear cut straight into Maximus's chest. The air left him, and he felt his fingers go numb. He clutched his knees tightly around the horse but found that he had no strength left. He flailed his arms and grabbed onto Sempronius's toga as he fell.

The ground hit him hard in the face, but it barely registered compared with the searing burn of the spear in his chest. It wasn't fair.

Sempronius tumbled to the ground beside Maximus. He stood and ripped his tunic from Maximus's feeble grasp.

Maximus took one last painful inhale. "There's more honor in death on this field than life in defeat," he said. His vision blurred and prickled with black spots. The last thing he saw was Sempronius retreating to the river and jumping on the

flat boat, the consular guards close at his heels. With that, a
curtain of blackness closed around him.

CHAPTER 40

Trebia River

Hannibal beat back the Romans until Scipio's legion had crumbled around him. The few who still fought were swiftly hacked to pieces. The Carthaginians were rabid for victory. They could smell it in the air around them. Hannibal led them in the final crushing blows.

His leg twinged with every step, but his father's words rang in his ears, propelling him forward. "Lion of Carthage! Lion of Carthage! Lion of Carthage!"

"Push them into the river," he shouted. "Keep only the officers alive." He nodded to Maherabal, who still rode at his side.

"Push them into the river!" Maherabal echoed to the Sacred Band. "Every officer is to be bound and held!"

Only one last feeble line of Romans stood between the Carthaginians and the river. Several Romans dropped their swords and spears into the water and jumped in after them. The Trebia ran red with their blood.

"They cannot take your honor! You are soldiers of Rome!" a voice came from nearby.

Hannibal looked over and saw young Scipio yelling for

his men to stand and fight for their honor. He smiled grimly. Was this the only Roman left who cared about honor? Scipio stood with a few dozen men to fight, but the Sacred Band hacked them down as easily as brittle tree branches.

Hannibal dashed into the midst of the Sacred Band, thrusting his sword through one Roman chest, then, another. He whirled to send his blade through another ill-trained Roman, and his blade met with the metal resistance of Scipio's well-managed weapon.

Hannibal twisted his sword in an upward motion and stabbed left.

Scipio blocked it. He held Hannibal in place for a moment. In a swift downward stroke, he tried to catch Hannibal on his bad leg, but Hannibal was faster, blocking the strike and countering with one of his own.

"So you are the Great Hannibal Barca," Scipio said.

"And you are a Roman without his back turned," Hannibal said. "Remarkable." He held the Roman's unblinking eyes before assailing him with an onslaught of steel and punches to the helmet.

Rather than becoming rattled and panicking, as Hannibal had expected, the Roman grew more steady and determined, countering Hannibal's vicious strokes with expertly placed defense. Hannibal came at him for several long minutes. While the Romans ran and the Sacred Band watched, Hannibal grudgingly admitted that this Roman was a worthy opponent. Nothing seemed to faze him.

"And I am Scipio the Younger."

Hannibal realized with surprise that this was the son of his father's nemesis.

In a sudden rapid movement, Scipio dodged left, whipped his sword back to catch Hannibal's weapon, and twisted his sword around it until Hannibal could either drop his sword or let his arm be broken.

The sword dropped from his hand. Before it could settle in the riverbank mud, Maherabal leaped behind Scipio and dashed him on the head with the hilt of his weapon, rendering him unconscious.

Scipio's eyes rolled back, and he dropped into the mud.

Maherabal bent to retrieve the fallen weapon from the mud. Hannibal took it from him somberly and looked around at the men who watched him, awaiting orders.

"Bring the captives to camp," Hannibal said. "Send Rome a message: their officers' lives in exchange for any supplies we need." He looked over at Scipio's unconscious form and pointed at him. "Bind that one extra carefully."

He mounted his horse and galloped back toward camp. Now that the battle was won, his leg throbbed. It would need to be dressed properly before it had time to get infected.

That night, the camp was full of modest celebration. They'd made it through the first battle on Roman soil with minimal losses. They'd decimated four legions of Roman soldiers. They should be proud. But they were men accustomed to battle and killing. While they would cheer and celebrate their glory, seasoned soldiers also knew the price they would pay for this battle today: nightmares born from hacking other humans to death. Whatever their reasons for fighting—money, fame, loyalty—each of them had signed up for this war knowing that it would be long and hard and costly, and in the end, they might not live to see their reward. So they measured each scrap of victory against the years of war ahead of them. Against the ghosts that would haunt their sleep.

CHAPTER 41

Barca Compound, Carthage

Sophonisba leaned against the balcony railing that overlooked the city skyline. White stone villas climbed the side of the hill. Little plumes of smoke feathered the air where sacrifices had been offered over open altars. In the distance, the stadium stood out above all else. Its half-hidden arches were like eyes surveilling the sea as if Yamm, the sea god, might unleash its wrath at any moment.

The baby kicked at Sophonisba's ribs incessantly these days, and she couldn't find a comfortable position no matter how hard she tried. When she sat, her back ached. When she stood, her legs wailed. Everything felt swollen. She wished Hannibal would hurry up and stuff swords down all the throats in Rome so he could come home to her. When she was pregnant with Hamilcar, he'd rubbed her back and whispered silly nonsense in her ear to make her laugh. Perhaps that's why little Hamilcar was such a charmer. He always had the right words to convince Grandma and Aunt Sapanibal and the maids into just about anything. She smiled. He sure was a handful, with his sweet dimples and warm, brown eyes.

The baby kicked again, harder this time.

Sophonisba sighed. She was entering her third trimester. What if Hannibal wasn't home by the time she was ready to give birth? It was useless to worry about this, she knew. If he could possibly make it home before her time, he would, and if he didn't, she would be fine. She'd done this before, and Lady Barca was here to help.

Sapanibal let herself out onto the balcony and flopped down on the daybed next to Sophonisba. As she leaned back, her eyes slid from her sister-in-law to the view of the city.

"The city is so quiet today," Sapanibal said.

Sophonisba studied the street beyond the balcony railing. The neighbors' children weren't screaming through the streets as was their custom, and there was a suspicious lack of merchant carts passing today. "I don't trust the quiet," she said.

Sapanibal wrinkled her nose at Sophonisba. "You're such a wet rag," she said. "I want to be happy."

Sophonisba turned her face away from the younger girl, hiding her raised eyebrows. Perhaps she was a wet rag, but it was not without reason.

Sapanibal sat up again. "What's it like to be married?"

"Tiring," Sophonisba said.

"I can't wait!" Sapanibal bounced a little on her seat. "I'll be a queen by spring!"

"Be careful of ambitious plans," Sophonisba said. "Timing of your marriage depends on a great number of things."

"The war should be long over by then. I don't see how it's so ambitious. It's at least four moon cycles away."

"Even if the war is finished by then, it will take at least one lunar cycle for the army to make it back to Carthage."

"Not if they sail here. I don't see why they have to climb those mountains again. You're so blue! Why don't you help me make a wedding gown?"

Lady Barca joined them on the balcony. Hamilcar ran circles around her legs while brandishing a wooden sword. "Enough of that talk, Sapanibal. There are much more pressing matters to attend to right now." She crossed to the railing and stood beside Sophonisba.

Hamilcar pointed his sword as he rushed at Sapanibal. "Charge!" he yelled.

"Hamilcar, no!" Sapanibal yelled in fake terror as he leaped on top of her and grabbed her armpits to tickle her. She put her arms around him and squeezed, laughing and blowing on his curls. They both rolled on the cushion, making enough noise to make up for the lack of it in the city this afternoon.

"I'm worried about our position in the Council," Lady Barca said. "With our men out of sight, our support is weakening by the day. The Hannas never miss an opportunity to gain the upper hand."

"Surely defeating Rome is more important to them than defeating the Barcas," Sophonisba said. "They can't possibly think they have anything to gain by badmouthing my husband."

"You have much to learn about Carthage and its politics. There are deep currents beneath these waters that have been churning long before Rome was founded."

"I'll leave the politics to you, then," Sophonisba said.

Lady Barca frowned. "That may not always be an option."

Sophonisba looked over at Lady Barca sharply. "Are you

sick?" She kept her voice low so that Sapanibal wouldn't overhear.

"No, of course not," Lady Barca rushed to say, "but I won't be alive forever, and it would be better if two of us in this household understood the situation." She looked over at Sapanibal who was crawling on the deck, chasing Hamilcar. "As the General's wife, you should be one of them."

"I will attend the Council meetings with you," Sophonisba said. She grimaced as the baby kicked again. Was it terrible of her that she had taken to comparing her unborn child with a horrid case of indigestion?

Lady Barca nodded. "Good."

They both looked out over the quiet city in silence.

CHAPTER 42

Cartagena

Cartagena was named after Carthage, but their similarities stopped there. Where Carthage shone like a pearl encapsulating her inhabitants in eternal paradise, Cartagena tossed buckets of water on her inhabitants whenever she pleased and turned brown and gray in the winter season. It made Hasdrubal restless for home, restless for a mission, restless to be anywhere but here. His presence here felt useless with the war taking place half a world away. His men were getting weary of the droopy weather and lack of purpose in their daily lives. They could only do so much drilling in a day before it started to all feel pointless.

Through the windows of his quarters, Hasdrubal held a prime view of Cartagena's damp city center. Farmers drove carts of hay and wool through the street on their way to the market. Donkeys brayed and defecated. Young boys, paid to keep the streets clean, chased after the droppings, scooping them into barrels that would be hauled outside the city at nightfall to fertilize the fields.

Hasdrubal paced from one window to the next. His troops, who camped just outside of the city, were nowhere to be seen from his windows. He knew that a few dozen men stood guard on the highest rooftops in the city. They would send up a cry if an enemy of Carthage was spotted, but otherwise, they were invisible.

The scribe looked up at him from the table in the corner of the room. "Sir?" the timid-looking man asked.

Hasdrubal turned his attention back to the task at hand. He was in the middle of composing a letter to Hannibal. He cleared his throat. "I know you have been pressing Carthage for needed supplies…" he thought for a moment, "but the Hannas are spreading rumors that are making it difficult to obtain the appropriate items. No, scratch that… Word from Carthage indicates that they are dragging their feet."

Hasdrubal sat down in a chair and, just as quickly, stood and paced to the opposite side of the room. "I have ordered my captains to make our men ready to follow your path into Italy."

He picked at a loose thread on his tunic for a moment and looked up again to see the scribe looking at him, waiting. "We can muster the needed supplies here in Cartagena and make the final push for Rome the moment we receive your command."

He wandered over to the map on the wall and studied the path from Cartagena across Iberia and down to Rome. Hannibal had sent word that it had been an arduous journey, but he was just as capable as his brother.

"Is that all, sir?" the scribe asked.

"Godspeed, Hasdrubal." Hasdrubal pressed his lips together, watching as the scribe etched the last words into the parchment, folded it, and sealed it with Hasdrubal's seal.

Hasdrubal crossed the room and picked up the letter. He left his quarters and crossed the town to the front gate. It wasn't raining anymore today and the sun tried to peek from behind the clouds.

At the front gate, he saw the messenger waiting on horseback. He handed over the letter and a bag of coins. As the man reached to take the money, Hasdrubal grabbed his wrist tightly. "Don't rest until it's in my brother's hands," he said.

"Yes, sir. Of course," the messenger said.

Hasdrubal let go of him.

As the messenger straightened on his horse, Hasdrubal reached out and smacked the horse's rump, sending him galloping away from the city.

Hasdrubal almost envied the man.

CHAPTER 43

217 BCE, Numidian Camp Outside Carthage

A fire burned outside of the tent, illuminating the red desert sand. There was nothing to see except the gentle slope of the black sand dunes in the distance and a few pointed lights from the city of Carthage a half-day's journey in the distance. The belt of the Milky Way glowed violet and blue, as if the gods were waving from the heavens, beckoning anyone who would listen.

No one looked up, however.

A Numidian Chieftain and his entourage surrounded the tent, silhouetted in the fire's weakening flames. The entourage held spears and entered the tent before the Chieftain.

Inside the small tent, a single candle flickered, lighting up the face of the man who held it. Ida Hanna stood and held both of his hands out to the Chieftain, a crafty smile spreading over his face.

"Scyla," Ida said. "Greetings."

Scyla did not smile. Instead, his shrewd eyes studied Ida's face, until Ida's solicitous smile melted away.

"Thank you for granting me this audience," Scyla said. He

cast his eyes around at his guards. "I risk my life being here."

"What is the nature of your danger?" Ida asked. Where in the brightness of daylight, Ida looked gangly and blustering, the shadows from the single flame sharpened the angles on his face and elongated his brow and nose, making him look fierce and powerful. The candle flamed a little higher for a brief flicker, illuminating the weapons of Ida's guards at his right and left shoulders.

"I come speaking treason against my king," Scyla said.

"Massinissa?" Ida asked.

"Massinissa is young and foolhardy. Numidia will embrace a new leader while he gallops around Italy dreaming of his own greatness."

"Massinissa is a fast and loyal ally who fights with my city. Why would I risk that security for you?" Ida asked.

A beat passed. Scyla narrowed his eyes and stepped closer so that the candle illuminated his face as well as Ida's. In a nearly indiscernible voice, he said, "I understand Massinissa is quite close to the Barca family. My messengers tell me that he is betrothed to the young Barca daughter. Under my leadership, Numidia would answer only to the Hannas."

Ida and Scyla held eyes for a moment. Then Ida raised his chin. "The Barcas will never see it coming," Ida said, a smile gleaming in his eyes.

CHAPTER 44

Carthaginian Camp, Present Day Italy

Forty captive Roman officers sat bound hand and foot in the dirt beneath the scanty shade of saplings. With their arms bound behind their back and their stomachs growling in hunger, they looked like ravenous dogs. They kicked and moaned as Hannibal stood before them, surrounded by a dozen members of his Sacred Band. The only officer who remained quiet was Scipio. He regarded Hannibal with solemn eyes, the only officer with an inkling of what was about to befall them.

Hannibal thought the Romans might negotiate. Carthage needed supplies, and Rome had already lost forty thousand soldiers. He had been wrong. Perhaps they weren't worried about losing another forty. Based on how they had fought in battle, the only officer who was more valuable to them in life was Scipio. They might have at least negotiated for Scipio. It would be a shame to kill such a worthy adversary.

He glared at the Roman filth around him. "We have received word from the Roman Senate regarding the terms for your release."

Several of the officers stopped kicking and stilled to listen to their fates.

"Their exact words were—" Hannibal cut his eyes to Maherabal, who cleared his throat.

"There is more honor in death than in negotiating with Carthage," Maherabal said in practiced Latin, holding out the Roman parchment in front of him.

Several of the captives spit in the direction of the Sacred Guard and renewed their struggle against their bindings, more frantically this time. Scipio again remained still, unsurprised by this verdict.

"It seems that your brothers have more valor in their Senate Chamber than when they're running from the battlefield," Hannibal said.

He stared at Scipio. "You," he said, pointing.

Scipio struggled to a standing position in his bindings.

Hannibal motioned him forward. "Walk with me," he said to Scipio.

One of the guards of the Sacred Band went forward and cut the ties around Scipio's ankles.

"Kill the rest," Hannibal said to the Sacred Band. He turned and walked away from the trees and the shrieks of the cowardly Romans toward the heart of the camp. He didn't untie Scipio's arms from behind his back, and Scipio didn't ask him to.

The sounds of sharp weapons hacking through flesh made Scipio shudder, but he remained otherwise stoic. Hannibal watched him glance back and saw a flicker of indecision, but the young man resisted the urge to try to sacrifice his life to save his men. It wouldn't have worked anyway, and Scipio must have known it.

They passed the medical tent where soldiers dressed each other's wounds and a fire pit where more soldiers stirred thin stew and hung their socks on lines of twine strung between tents. Many of them looked up from their tasks to the General, hoping he had walked by to bring them word of supplies from Rome. They'd been going without many necessities for too long.

"You were the last Roman fighting," Hannibal said, turning to study his young nemesis. Something about Scipio's near fight to the death forced Hannibal to respect the younger man. He was the son of a soldier, a man who would slay an animal with his bare hands if that's what it took to live. Hannibal wanted to hate him, but he couldn't.

"So I was," Scipio said. "Your guard hit me from behind before I could kill you."

"My enemies usually die." Hannibal glanced in the direction of the slaughter that was now finished. Case in point. "I want you to return to Rome and tell them about the battle. Tell them of the forty thousand Roman lives that were lost, including the officers they declined to save. Tell them of the five thousand Carthaginian losses. No doubt you will tell them we are desperate for reinforcements and supplies, but let me remind you that we are no worse off than we were before we slashed through four Roman legions."

Scipio considered this for a moment before responding. "I fail to see the strategy in my release. My knowledge in Rome gives you no advantage."

Had the words sounded cocky, Hannibal might have struck him down then and there, but Scipio only stated the facts.

"I have hated Rome my whole life," Hannibal said. "Rome is a greedy bastard grubbing for what doesn't belong to it."

Scipio said nothing. *Wise*, thought Hannibal, and then said, "But you are not Rome."

"You will not make me a traitor," Scipio said.

Hannibal's temper rose, but he tamped it down. Perhaps that would have been a better idea than letting him go, but no. Even if he could persuade Scipio to play traitor, he would never trust him. "No. You would be a fool to believe that of me. I am a man of honor. As a soldier, when it ends, that's all that remains. And I would be remiss if I couldn't recognize honor even among my enemies. You were the only honorable Roman on the Trebia River field."

Scipio frowned at these words, but he didn't try to argue in defense of the Romans' honor. "How do you benefit?"

"A worthy adversary. I spared Rome's only fine soldier. If I lose, my name will not become a joke." Was he making the right decision? Was he losing the war with this single decision? But if he didn't have his honor, what did he have?

Hannibal took out his dagger and slashed the bindings from Scipio's wrists. He motioned for a soldier nearby to bring a horse, and he handed the reins over to Scipio.

"I look forward to meeting you in battle in the future," Scipio said.

Hannibal nodded curtly. "Godspeed."

Scipio mounted the horse and turned to Hannibal. He nodded once and then kicked the horse to spur it toward Rome.

CHAPTER 45

Rome

Scipio returned to Rome to find the confidence of the Roman citizens faltering. Unofficial accounts of the lost battle had circled the city and the surrounding countryside, sending even the least religious of them into a fit of sacrificial prayer and contemplation. The Senate had led them to believe that Rome could not lose a battle to Carthage, but it turned out that the one thing that couldn't happen was the very thing that had.

Scipio stood before the Senate with Sempronius at his left. Of the Senators, these two were the only ones to return from the battlefield. They were the leaders of the debate by default.

"The element of surprise is all that worked in Hannibal's favor," Sempronius said. "His army is numerically inferior, and now they lack enough food and resources to nourish their march to Rome. Give me the two legions now protecting Rome, and we will erase this parasite from our countryside."

A few Senators murmured their agreement. It was easy for them to agree with Sempronius considering his advantage of age and experience.

Scipio raised his arm to draw their attention back to himself. "Hannibal's army is superior to our remaining force in every way. Numbers are hardly a factor when his casualty rate is one to every six of ours. We will not outguess Hannibal. All we can hope to do is outlast him."

The room was quiet for a moment, with everyone looking from Sempronius's glower to Scipio's steady expression.

"And how, young Scipio, do you plan on outlasting Hannibal Barca?" one of the senators asked.

Scipio felt some trepidation at what he planned to propose. After all, Hannibal had spared his life. But now was not a time to grow weak. "Carthage is not sending the necessary reinforcements to Rome, indicating that support for this campaign at home is breaking down. If we attack the city directly, it will rip itself apart."

The room exploded with chatter.

"Attack Carthage with Hannibal and his army ten days' march from Rome?" one senator called out.

"We must mimic Hannibal's tactics if we hope to defeat him," Scipio said.

"The sole surviving captive from Trebia admires Hannibal's tactics," Sempronius said, his voice booming over all of the others. "How can we trust you? What kind of deal have you struck to keep your life?"

The accusation was no surprise. He knew it was only a matter of time before they wondered about the truth of his story. They never wanted to listen to him to begin with. "To not recognize genius in your enemy is to be blind to victory," Scipio said.

"No one can question Scipio's honor or courage in battle,"

a mild-mannered senator said. He'd known Scipio from birth and had watched him train from a young age. His words seemed to breathe sense into the rest of the room, and the other senators nodded.

"We will need more than two legions to defeat the Carthaginians at any rate," Scipio said. "Give me permission to raise an army and I will leave half of that army here to defend Rome."

A few of the senators agreed.

Scipio looked around the room, noting that they looked to Sempronius for their cue on what to say. Sempronius stood stone-faced next to Scipio, reluctant both to disagree with sensible advice and to lose face to a youth who had bested him in battle and strategy.

"Let's call a vote," the mild-mannered senator said. "All in favor of having Scipio raise an army, say aye."

The room echoed with ayes.

"Anyone not in favor, say nay."

There was only a smattering of nays.

"Then it is settled," Sempronius barked. "Scipio will raise an army and I will lead the remaining two legions to the north to confront Hannibal and slow his advance. Meeting adjourned." He pressed his lips together and left the room.

CHAPTER 46

Council Chamber, Carthage

Lady Barca sat between Sophonisba and Sapanibal in the Council Chamber. This wasn't a regularly scheduled meeting. Ida had called it only last night. To his right sat a young man she had never seen before. By his clothing and his stance, he looked like a chieftain. A sense of foreboding trickled through Lady Barca's middle. Whatever Ida had up his sleeve could not be good news for Carthage. Or the Barcas.

Ida stood and held his hands up, calling the meeting to order. His haughty eyes met Lady Barca's for a quick moment before slipping away. When the room was quiet, he spoke. "I called this emergency council meeting today in response to the happenings in our neighboring kingdom of Numidia."

Sophonisba shifted and her brow puckered.

Sapanibal gasped at the mention of her future kingdom.

Ida smirked at them both and continued. "We are well aware of the recent struggle over the crown, but the nobles of Numidia have risen with one voice to proclaim Scyla the new King of Numidia."

Much of the chamber clapped as Scyla stood and bowed his head to the Council.

"Massinissa," Sapanibal whispered. She fidgeted in her seat.

"It is a pleasure to be welcomed in the chamber of my kingdom's greatest friend," Scyla said.

Lady Barca stood and the pretender's eyes snapped to her face. Anger filled her at this sudden development. Didn't Ida know anything? "This is an outrage," she exclaimed.

Scyla cut a gaze in Ida's direction, as though he had not been expecting any objections to his announcement. "I don't understand," he said.

Ida glared at Lady Barca, and she glared right back. "I will not sit idly by and listen to this pretender while the rightful king of Numidia is campaigning with Carthage's army in Italy."

"Watch your tongue, woman!" Ida snapped. "This is a powerful and respected friend. The Numidian nobles have accepted Scyla as the rightful king of their country, and Carthage does too."

"Nobles can be purchased," Lady Barca said. She raised her brows pointedly at Ida. "Can't they, Ida? This man must have made you some big promises, but you do not speak for all of Carthage. I will not recognize this man as king of anything until the rightful king returns to defend this usurpation."

"I will not take such hollow threats from a mere woman," Scyla said imperiously. "You will die of old age before our soldiers return. This war is a waste of our valuable resources."

"And you will die of old age before a speck of honor touches your blood," Lady Barca said coldly. "A true king would have challenged the king to his face."

Scyla's eyes flashed with fury. He glared first at Lady Barca and then in Ida's direction as he stormed from the chamber, letting the heavy chamber doors crash shut behind him.

Everyone in the council chamber jumped to their feet yelling. A few yelled at Ida, but most leveled their accusations against Lady Barca.

Lady Barca let them yell. She would not back down. There was no honor in this betrayal.

"That was the king of Numidia," Ida shouted over everyone else. He slammed his palms against the table as he spoke. "Even a Barca must be held responsible for their actions."

"An immediate apology!" someone shouted.

"Now we'll be at war with Numidia, too!" someone else shouted.

The chamber broke out in even more animated yelling.

Sapanibal watched wide-eyed as her dream of being the future queen of Numidia went up in smoke. She twisted her hands into her sash and looked to Lady Barca for solace.

Sophonisba pressed her lips together in restrained anger and held a hand to her middle. Lady Barca could imagine her fury. Numidia was her homeland, and her loyalty wouldn't be so swiftly swayed by Ida Hanna.

Geromachus looked on from a corner of the table in perturbed silence. He had always been a voice of reason for the Council, but today he only watched, a worried look etched into his wrinkled face.

"I call for immediate reparations," Ida exclaimed, pointing his thin finger at Lady Barca's face.

The yelling in the room dampened as everyone waited for Lady Barca's next words. "The Barca family will not support Scyla. We will actively support Massinissa's return to the throne of Numidia."

She tapped Sophonisba and Sapanibal, who stood and exited with her through the back door.

The chamber room rumbled after the Barcas left, and for a moment, no one held the floor. Geromachus considered speaking in Lady Barca's defense. She was his oldest friend, and there was no one more loyal to Carthage. But he sensed that his hands were tied. The majority was no longer in favor of the Barcas and he knew that any compromise he struck must favor Ida Hanna and his supporters. There was a day when Carthage was proud to defend itself, its allies, and its resources and wouldn't have stood for such blatant treachery. Lady Barca was right; Ida Hanna was supporting treason, and Scyla was surely promising the Hannas Numidia's support in return.

But, Geromachus reminded himself, for a long time now, it had only been a matter of time before Ida figured out how to bring Hannibal down. Ida had always been both self-important and persuasive.

Ida pounded his fist on the table to bring the Council's attention back to himself. "This arrogance cannot be tolerated. We are not the kingdom of Barca. We must resolve to punish this disrespect. I move to recall Hannibal as General of the army in Italy."

The chamber erupted with shouts of agreement.

Geromachus stood slowly, painfully, and a hush fell over the room. He cleared his throat, hating the compromise that must be struck, but knowing that the alternative was far worse. "Reparations should be made, yes. But recalling a successful general in the middle of a campaign is too far." He wet his lips and forged ahead. "There was a marriage arranged for the Barca girl to be married to the king of Numidia. We should decree that that marriage be upheld…with the new king of Numidia."

"Yes," someone called out. "Tie our countries together through marriage."

Ida frowned, no doubt calculating whether marrying the Barca girl would turn Scyla's loyalties to the Barcas. Then, he smiled wickedly. "A show of hands to decree that this edict is to be followed on pain of exile from Carthage."

The hands of most of the Council shot up in the air, and the rest followed after a beat. There was no better compromise.

Ida smiled. "The decree has passed."

Geromachus sank back to his seat. Lady Barca had once told him that she would rather die than be dishonorable to her city and to all that her husband had fought to preserve. How would he convince her to defy her sense of honor and marry her daughter to a Numidian imposter? Victory was impossible. Survival might be.

He felt the weariness of his age and position sink deeply into his bones and for the hundredth time in the past few months was grateful not to be a young man just beginning in the world, trying to make sense of the madness.

CHAPTER 47

Carthaginian Camp, Umbria

The Umbrian countryside sprawled with vineyards and farms, sheep and cattle. The sun's gentle glow warmed the ground and deepened the greens of the waving grasses. The hills spread out warm and freshly washed like pillows for the gods. In the distance, a small but imposing hilltop town made of orange tufa bricks blended into the side of a plateau. Pigeons cooed as they flew to and from holes carved in the sides of the plateau.

Hannibal looked up from the map he'd spread out on a makeshift table in front of his tent in time to see a lone man approaching on horseback.

Maherabal and Massinissa were bent over the table with him as he detailed the next step in his plan. They, too, looked up.

The man halted in front of Hannibal and climbed down from his horse.

Hannibal stepped closer.

"I bring you a message from your brother," the messenger said.

Hannibal frowned. He thought he was clear the last time

when he told Hasdrubal to stop sending him letters. It was far too dangerous.

Hannibal took the letter from the messenger and read it. His frown deepened. His brother was expecting orders to march to Italy. Fool. Hannibal growled. "No," he said. "This cannot be allowed." He grabbed the messenger's arms. "Turn now and race back to Hasdrubal. Tell him to stay in Iberia. Tell him not to abandon our escape or the defense of Carthage. And tell him to stop sending letters. This country is thick with Roman spies." He dropped the messenger's arms.

"Let me write it down," the messenger said.

"No! Italy is unsafe enough as it is. You can remember. All you have to tell him is no," Hannibal said. "Now go!"

The messenger climbed quickly back onto his horse and kicked it to a run.

Hannibal ran a hand through his hair. He knew that Hasdrubal was bored and tired of waiting around, but he had to understand that his position was vitally important. With each letter he sent he sounded more and more likely to follow Hannibal to Italy on a whim. He growled, wishing he could give his brother a solid smack before he did anything stupid.

He turned to see Massinissa beckoning to him frantically and jogged back over to the table.

"Hannibal!" Massinissa said. "I just got word that two Roman legions have snuck between our scouts. They're moving quickly and will have secured the parallel valley by this evening."

"It's too late to get out," Maherabal said. His calmness contrasted with Massinissa's nervous energy. "They'll have us surrounded."

"Should we prepare fortifications?" Massinissa asked.

Hannibal shook his head. He had anticipated that this might happen and had created a solution that was just odd enough to work. "No," he said. "I have a plan. We need firewood and this village's cattle."

Massinissa's eyes widened as if he thought Hannibal was joking, but Maherabal sprang into action.

CHAPTER 48

Umbria

Night had fallen. A Roman scout sat in the upper branches of a tree, watching the dark landscape around him for any sign of movement from the Carthaginian army. His ankles were sore from holding his perch for so long, and he wondered how much longer he would have to sit here. The consul, Sempronius, had been certain that Hannibal's army would move tonight, and the hours of darkness were slipping away.

A spark of orange caught his eye. He turned to stare at it. Another spark trailed after it and another until he could clearly see a line of brightly glowing torches moving single file up from the valley where the Carthaginians camped and up onto the ridge line.

The scout leaned forward. This must be it, at last! He swung himself down from the tree, landing on his feet. His ankles cracked with relief.

He leaped onto his horse and raced back to the Roman camp.

As he galloped into camp, Sempronius' fierce eyes fell on him like a hungry dog expecting a hunk of half-rotten meat.

"Confirmed movement from the Carthaginian camp," the

scout said, breathless. "Hundreds of torches moving south out of the valley and over the ridge line."

Sempronius smiled, but the smile didn't reach his eyes. He was a man who was in this for blood and revenge. He didn't like looking stupid and Hannibal had made him look like a downright fool at Trebia.

The scout backed up a few steps.

"Move now!" Sempronius shouted. "Both legions intercept Hannibal along his southern escape route." He swung up onto his horse while the Roman soldiers frantically formed their marching lines.

The scout fell into his place in line and legions began their race to catch the Carthaginians. His heart beat faster, and his palms grew sweaty. Maybe he would be the scout whose words would win Rome the war. But then again, Hannibal was, by most accounts, a cunning general. If this assault was successful, he may be a hero. If this was a trap, Sempronius would kill him for being wrong.

He thought about his lover at home. Would she be proud of him or ashamed she ever knew him? Would she hear anything at all about him? And what of his wife and children?

Many frantic minutes passed as the Roman army charged. Then, a cry went up from the front of the line.

Hero, he thought. This was it.

Men in front of him released their spears, and he prepared to do the same, the moment the men in front of him fell back.

There was loud commotion ahead and the shuffling of heavy footfall, but zero visibility into the enemy line. Unable to see a Carthaginian to aim at, the scout wound up and released his spear at a moving torch before him. It wasn't until the spear had left his hand that he realized the torches in front of him were not terrified Carthaginians caught off guard, but stampeding cattle running in opposite directions, trying to avoid the spears. His stomach dropped. This was all his fault.

The scout's spear pierced the shoulder of a cow and dropped it to its knees. The flaming wood attached to its horns sank into the brush beside the trail, smoking in the grass for a moment before lighting a dead tree on fire.

Several Romans around him dismounted and moved closer to inspect the deception.

Sempronius barged his way to the front of the line. "What is going on here?" he shouted, but he fell silent when he saw that the line of torches extending along the ridge wasn't men holding torches but cows with flaming wood tied to their horns. He threw his sword down in the dirt.

"Find them," Sempronius barked. "They can't be far. Then move both legions toward Rome to assume defensive positions."

CHAPTER 49

Umbria

Hannibal followed the Umbrian scout through the dark swampland. The army followed behind him with only the muted noise of boots moving through mud. A waning crescent moon cast a weak glow on the desolate marsh around them. There were no trees, no animals, no crickets. The only traces of life were the scrubby brush, which looked dead, and the occasional squawk of a frog. Swarms of gnats and mosquitoes feasted on any exposed flesh.

Hannibal leaned toward the scout. "Exit the marsh at the southwest point," he whispered. "We plan to ambush Sempronius on his return to Rome."

"At Lake Trasimene?" the scout asked.

"Yes."

"No man has passed through this marsh in a hundred years, much less an army," the local scout said. "You plan to move quick enough to lay ambush to two legions passing on the Appian Way?"

Of course it sounded crazy when he put it like that, Hannibal thought. The Appian Way was a major highway for much of Rome's trade and the most direct road into Rome.

"This path has no ice," Hannibal said. He spurred his horse to go faster and moved ahead of the scout.

CHAPTER 50

Lake Trasimene

Massinissa watched Sempronius march with his legions through the narrow pass beside Lake Trasimene. What had the Umbrian scout called it? The White Rock Pass? That sounded right. White rock faces tapered down toward the path and plummeted again on the other side of the path directly down into the lake.

From his position on the cliff, there was little danger that Sempronius or any of his scouts would see Massinissa, even if they looked up. One of his Numidian captains stood next to him.

"Will we charge after they pass?" the captain asked.

"No," Massinissa said. "Only when they begin their retreat toward us." He drew back from the ledge and glanced behind him as his cavalry lined up in battle-ready formation. The horses pawed at the ground, antsy to move again, but the men were still, waiting for the command. In this battle, timing would be key.

Massinissa had doubted the wisdom of this plan, but Hannibal had succeeded on far crazier schemes. Still, he glanced over his shoulder just to be sure the Romans hadn't snuck up behind him. He realized that his fists were knotted and flattened them against his thighs. Not every sound was a Roman, he told himself. Hannibal would have planned for it. He wondered if even the most war-hardened soldiers had steel nerves before the start of a fresh battle.

CHAPTER 51

Lake Trasimene

Hannibal heard the Roman legions marching along the path. They weren't trying to be quiet about it. Their footsteps rang off the cliff walls, announcing that they were just around the corner.

The Carthaginian army stood at the ready in the middle of the road waiting for the word to charge.

"Steady, men, wait for their charge," Hannibal said.

A second later, the first Roman legion turned the corner, led by Sempronius. Sempronius's eyes widened in shock, and he hesitated.

"Hannibal," he said.

Hannibal smiled grimly and motioned for the forces waiting atop the cliffs to push boulders down the hills. The great rocks fell, smashing into the rear ranks of the Roman army and confusing them. Some retreated, and some pushed forward.

"Charge!" Sempronius yelled, kicking his horse forward and trying to shove through the Carthaginian block in front of him. He pulled his sword and led his men, swiping his blade back and forth, hitting very few of the well-trained

Carthaginians at the front line. He didn't look like a soldier so much as a trapped animal desperate for survival.

The Carthaginian soldiers closest to him yanked him from his mount and savaged him with steel.

More boulders fell on the Roman ranks, pushing them down the hill toward the lake.

"Toward the lake!" Hannibal yelled, leading his men down the steep hill to trap the Romans near the lake.

Many of the Romans, seeing Sempronius fall, dropped their weapons and fled in the opposite direction. Others dashed toward the lake, perhaps hoping to swim across it. To make it across, they would have to drop their weapons. *Let them try*, Hannibal thought.

Hannibal focused his energy on slashing down any man attempting to make it to the lake. Within minutes, the Romans lost hope and fled back up the road.

The Carthaginian soldiers' chase was brief, punctuated by a charge from Massinissa's cavalry that decimated Rome's numbers and blocked any hope of escape.

Roman blood spilled freely, and Hannibal cut through one retreating soldier after another. It was like chopping down a forest of cowardly trees. Many of them had forgotten that they had weapons at all, and went down with nothing more than a scream of terror and half-hearted swings of their fists.

Eventually, Hannibal met Massinissa in the middle of the battle. They exchanged a nod and turned to begin the final push down the hill and into the lake. They would take no survivors today.

When all that remained were Carthaginians, the men faced the pink-tinged lake and celebrated their victory. Two more enemy legions were gone, with very few casualties on their own side.

Hannibal looked up at Massinissa.

"Another of your schemes worked," the Numidian king said.

"Why do you sound surprised?" Hannibal asked.

CHAPTER 52

216 BCE, Barca Compound, Carthage

Lady Barca followed a servant into the front hall. Geromachus greeted her, and she met his greeting with an icy one of her own. She knew he would come. He must have struck a compromise with the Council, and by the careful look on his face, she could tell that she wasn't going to like it.

"Is there somewhere we might speak privately?" he asked.

She narrowed her eyes, wishing she could send him away. But they had been friends for many years. "Come with me." She turned and led him into a sitting room with windows facing out to the sea. It was dark now, and the city was quiet.

She shut the sitting room door so that no one in the family would hear them.

Geromachus sat on the cushioned seat, watching Lady Barca as she stood sideways next to the window. She wanted to turn her back on whatever he had to say, but she couldn't be rude. The silence stretched taut between them.

"Don't lose Carthage over Numidia," he finally said.

"As I mentioned at the meeting, my position is decided," she said. She turned to him. "I was offended by your lack of support."

Geromachus had the grace to look down. He stood with effort and paced the few steps to stand next to her at the window.

"I bought us the only compromise that would save this war."

"Which is?"

"The Hannas are much stronger than you imagine," he said instead of answering her question. "The Barca men have long been at war in Iberia or Italy, too far away to stop the Hannas from swaying public ear."

"I believe I've held the Barca position as well as any man," Lady Barca snapped, unable to keep the anger from her tone.

"But you're not a general. Carthage is poor from this war, and who knows if there will be any immediate payoff if we win it?"

"You mean beyond the immediate payoff of sacking Rome? Only a fool could be so short-sighted."

"You are right," he conceded. "But, the Council is not made up of philosophers. They are used to getting what they want as soon as they want it. To them, the battle is out of sight, and they cannot justify the sacrifices we are making on its behalf."

"Ida Hanna won't get away with this. The second Hannibal returns he will lose any support he had," she said, but the words sounded weak even to her ears.

Geromachus reached out and took her hand. She was angry with him, but still, it was a comfort. He was the only ally she had against Ida, but even he wasn't strong enough to sway the entire Council. They were alone until her sons returned.

"I have no doubt Barca will seize back the Council if they

return," Geromachus said. "But in order for that to happen, we must make allowances to gain their continued support. Carthage will not remain loyal to the Barcas without it."

Lady Barca pulled her hand away. For the first time since the meeting, she felt her composure slip and the weight on her chest grew heavier. Tears pricked at her eyes and she covered her face with her hands.

"How are some men so fickle when some are so strong?" she asked, her voice wavering. "This isn't the noble city my husband defended. Why do we sacrifice for a city that has no memory, no loyalty?"

Geromachus touched her arm briefly. "Those are questions only the truly wise may ever answer."

Lady Barca wiped the tears from her eyes and took a deep breath, regaining her stony composure. "What must we do?" she asked.

"Your daughter's marriage to the king of Numidia must continue as planned," he said, hesitating before finishing his sentence. "To the new king of Numidia."

Lady Barca drew in a sharp breath. "No…," she said, her voice hovering for a moment before quivering into the night. Even as she breathed the word, she knew there was no other option. Geromachus wouldn't have asked if there was one.

He turned and let himself out of the sitting area.

Lady Barca turned back to the window. To relent was to eschew the honor she had sworn to all her life. To refuse was to condemn her family and her city to a certain end. There were no other options.

For one moment, she sank into the bowels of despair that threatened to drown her. She felt powerless. If she could no longer protect her family, what was next? A tear slid down her cheek and dripped onto her robe.

Squeezing her eyes shut tightly, she shook her head. She imagined her husband's face, his jaw set, and his eyes flaming. She'd seen this expression many times, and it was the one she pictured when his last moments were described to her. He had known he would die, and he hadn't backed down. The image strengthened her. When she opened her eyes, her determination had returned. There was one more duty she must face. She knew what she must do.

CHAPTER 53

Campagna, Present Day Italy

Scipio sat in the litter with the Magistrate of Campagna, mostly ignoring the beautiful countryside of southern Italy and trying to ignore how hot he felt under his full armor. This was the magistrate's weekly trip into the country to clear his lungs and stay in touch with the farming community. Never mind that the official never actually left the litter. But Scipio wouldn't complain. In the last few weeks, he'd grown accustomed to indulging powerful old men if it meant they would give him the army and supplies he needed. It was a complicated game of latrones.

He was almost done raising his army. He needed the Magistrate in Campagna to provide him ten thousand men. Then he would have all the men he needed to launch his two-pronged attack on Hannibal's forces near Rome and the city of Carthage.

"The Senate usually demands conscription," the Magistrate said. "I've never had a general come to personally request soldiers."

"We could demand soldiers," Scipio said, "but the ones we conscript aren't always desirable. I've come to ask for Campagna's best."

"We are not a bellicose people," the Magistrate said, as though this settled things.

"Rome's survival is at stake," Scipio said. "As your ally, we could ask for nothing more."

The Magistrate thought for a moment, looking sideways at Scipio.

Scipio forced his spine even straighter under the Magistrate's scrutiny. A drop of sweat slid from underneath his helmet and down the back of his neck. He'd made his play. Now he hoped that the Magistrate would take the bait.

"How many do you need?" the Magistrate asked.

"I've asked for ten thousand from every district. Each has been accommodating," Scipio said.

"Seventy thousand men? Are you taking over the world?"

"It's enough to fortify Rome and invade Africa at the same time," Scipio said. "It's ambitious, but it's the only way we can be certain of Rome's protection."

The Magistrate thought for another long moment. Finally, he said, "It will be done."

Scipio shook his hand and jumped off the litter. A soldier brought him his horse, and he galloped toward Rome.

CHAPTER 54

Barca Compound, Carthage

Lady Barca watched Sophonisba nurse tiny baby Didobal from the doorway. A new grandchild filled her with both joy and sadness. She wished that her son would come home to see his new daughter and put everything in Carthage right again, but she knew this was nothing more than idle dreaming. Hannibal was far away outside of Rome, and Ida Hanna was here in Carthage, determined to overthrow all that the Barcas had labored to preserve.

And she must do what she vowed never to do.

She sighed.

Sophonisba looked up. "She's sleeping," she said. "Come hold her."

Lady Barca entered the room and gathered Didobal into her arms. Tiny black lashes rested on her wrinkled face. Already she seemed to have her mother's thick curly hair and delicately curved mouth.

A servant peeked her head into the room. "Anything I can get for you, Lady Barca?"

Lady Barca looked up at the servant. "Go get Sapanibal," she said.

"You're not planning to marry her off to the pretender, are you?" Sophonisba asked, her black eyes flashing with anger.

Lady Barca couldn't bring herself to speak yet and waited for Sapanibal. She didn't want to say the words more than once.

"You sent for me," Sapanibal said as she entered the room. Her face had lost some of its frivolity, and she looked very serious in that moment.

"Sapanibal. Come, sit here by the window. We have something we need to discuss."

Sapanibal did as Lady Barca asked, folding her hands in her lap as she sat. She bit her lip. "What is it?" she asked. "We've been worried."

Lady Barca passed the baby back to Sophonisba and paced from one side of the room to the other. She felt like a trapped bird, and she knew that the feeling wasn't likely to pass. She paused in the middle of the room where she had the best view of them both. "I choose to tell both of you this news at the same moment because it will be the two of you who must deal with the future together."

"Sure we will all deal with it together," Sophonisba said.

Lady Barca pressed her lips together and continued. "There is a time when one must place family and state above oneself. Sapanibal, what I ask of you is as a matron of Carthage and the matriarch of this family."

"Yes, Mother," Sapanibal said.

Lady Barca crossed to where Sapanibal sat at the window seat and took her hand. "You are to marry Scyla, the king of Numidia." She worked hard to keep the contempt from her voice as she said the name.

Sapanibal drew her hand back as though from a flame.

"Massinissa is the king of Numidia," Sophonisba protested. "How could you do this?"

Lady Barca looked sharply at Sophonisba, who was sitting upright in bed now. "This decision is not for your happiness, or mine, but for the good of the city. For the good of Barca."

Sophonisba pulled her hand to her cheek, a reflex to the blood rushing to her head.

Lady Barca turned her attention back to Sapanibal. "You must ensure our family's survival and the continued support of your brothers at war. If you don't, they will die, and all of Carthage will be lost to Rome." She felt another protest about to break from Sophonisba's lips and held up her hand to stop it. "I have thought long about this reality. It is the only way we survive."

Sapanibal stared up at Lady Barca, eyes wide. Gone was her youthful excitement about her future Queenship of Numidia, and in its place rested fear.

Perhaps she appreciates the gravity of the situation, Lady Barca thought. But it pained her that it had to happen this way, and she could only pray that Sapanibal's spirit wouldn't be crushed under the weight of war's sacrifice.

"You will do as I say," Lady Barca said.

"Yes, mother," Sapanibal said. Tears sprang from her eyes and dropped down her cheeks.

Didobal started screaming, as though the anger and fear in the room were too much to bear.

Lady Barca kissed Sapanibal's head and then motioned for her to leave the room. She shut the door behind her daughter and closed her eyes. She was grateful that the baby's shrieks provided a moment of distraction for Sophonisba. When the baby had calmed, Lady Barca opened her eyes.

"This is outrageous!" Sophonisba said, struggling to keep her voice low so that she didn't upset the baby. "Hannibal would never stand for this."

Lady Barca glared at her. "Hannibal is not here. We must survive."

"How is breaking an alliance with the rightful king of Numidia and giving in to Ida Hanna's demands surviving? You betray your word. Death would be better."

Lady Barca's temper flared. Sophonisba had no idea what this decision was costing her. She'd lived her entire life believing that she would never betray her word, that only weak people found themselves in such a situation, and now she was being forced to either give up her honor or sacrifice everything else she held dear.

"Hannibal has been gone for a long time," Lady Barca said. "You saw how ready the council was to turn their loyalty to Ida. They don't understand the importance of this war anymore."

"Make them understand," Sophonisba said.

"I have tried, but unless they see a complete and miraculous victory over Rome in the next few days, there's nothing I can do. They're on the verge of pulling all support from Hannibal. Giving in to this one thing will buy us more time to win."

"What of Massinissa when he finds out?" Sophonisba continued. "Without a country to back him, he'll abandon Hannibal on the field. Have you thought about what that could mean for Carthage?"

"Have you?" Lady Barca snapped. "If Scyla is not appeased, Carthage will be gone before Hannibal can return, and your baby girl will never live to walk and talk."

A long silence stretched between them.

"He *will* return," Sophonisba said quietly. "What will we tell him when he does?"

"That we had no other choice," Lady Barca said. Not able to bear any more questions or accusations, she turned and walked from the room, her feet falling heavily on the floor as though she was an iron waiting to be dropped into the sea.

As she passed by Sapanibal's chamber, she heard the girl sobbing quietly and desperately, as if the world had come to an end. Maybe it had. Perhaps she was wise to cry now. She was, after all, little more than a pawn in someone else's giant political scheme, Lady Barca thought bitterly. That's all Ida Hanna saw any of them as. But at least she could rest in the knowledge that he wouldn't have the last word this time.

CHAPTER 55

Carthage Ceremonial Hall

The enormous state hall held bouquets of pink and orange hibiscus blossoms draped with chains of pearls. Incense wafted from the altar at the front of the hall, where the priest of Baal knelt for the ceremonial animal sacrifice. Sapanibal wore the same dress Lady Barca had worn thirty years ago in her wedding to General Hamilcar. It was Carthage purple, embroidered in pearl beads and glimmering diamonds.

Sophonisba bit back a grimace. *This wedding doesn't require an animal sacrifice; Sapanibal is the sacrifice,* Sophonisba thought.

Sapanibal stood hand in hand with Scyla, putting on a brave face in front of hundreds of Carthage's most elite citizens. The rest of the city waited in the streets for the trumpets to signify that the marriage was official before gods and country.

Everyone who mattered in Carthage was present for the wedding of Sapanibal Barca, daughter of the great General Hamilcar Barca, and Scyla, the presumed king of Numidia. All smiled and clapped at the appropriate times, excited to move on to the feasting and dancing that would follow the ceremony.

The only thing Sophonisba felt grateful for right now was that Sapanibal had taken a sudden, rapid interest in world politics and had thrown herself desperately into her studies over the last few weeks. Instead of obsessing over her gown or hair or idly dreaming of her strange new husband-to-be, she had memorized the names and titles of Numidia's nobles and the origins of all of Carthage's and Numidia's imports and exports. It was as if throwing herself into studying could somehow save her.

You must ensure our family's survival and the continued support of your brothers at war. If you don't, they will die, and all of Carthage will be lost to Rome. The words thrummed in Sophonisba's mind, and she imagined that they must ring even louder and more frighteningly in Sapanibal's. Sophonisba bit the insides of her cheeks. It wasn't fair! Sapanibal was barely more than a child; she shouldn't have to atone for the mistakes of an entire city. But more than that, Sophonisba was still angry with Lady Barca, who had insisted that this was the only solution and then refused to attend the wedding. Her excuse was that she had a headache. She'd looked every one of her sixty years of age, but that didn't make it right for her to force her daughter into a marriage that benefitted Ida Hanna's political climb and then refuse to even show up for it. How weak! Sophonisba clenched her fists.

Ida Hanna seemed to know that Lady Barca was not coming. He whispered something to the officiant, and the ceremony started precisely on time, which heaped more fuel on Sophonisba's rage. How dare he not wait on the mother of the bride, even if she claimed to be ill? As the ceremony started, some members of the council looked at Sophonisba and frowned. They, too, wondered why they weren't waiting for Lady Barca, but no one said anything. Sophonisba didn't either. What could she say? The hall was lined with the Hannas' armed guards.

The couple knelt before the altar and the priest of Baal put a gold crown on Scyla's head, and then on Sapanibal's.

"I pronounce you the King and Queen of Numidia," the priest said, his brassy voice echoing through the hall.

They stood and turned to face the audience as man and wife, king and queen.

Scyla smirked and nodded.

Sapanibal's lips bent upward, but her eyes remained wide and petrified.

Sophonisba glanced to her right and saw Ida standing to clap, glowing radiantly as though he should have been the blushing bride. She sucked back a growl and stood with the crowd, clapping mechanically. She felt like the only person in the hall, besides Sapanibal, who wasn't overjoyed by this moment.

"We've just had the great privilege of witnessing history," someone behind Sophonisba said.

"Indeed," someone else responded. "But I wonder if this means the Barcas are handing over power to the Hannas."

The crowd parted as the king and queen walked forward and down the middle of the room. The audience threw hibiscus blossoms and pinches of salt at the couple. Sapanibal's eyes filled with momentary panic as she searched the crowd.

Her eyes met Sophonisba's. Sophonisba was angry that this was happening, but it wasn't the girl's fault. She summoned a smile and nodded in encouragement, and a look of relative calm returned to Sapanibal's features.

If Lady Barca were here right now, she would see what a mistake this was, Sophonisba thought. She would have to figure out something else. Her anger spiked anew.

CHAPTER 56

Barca Compound, Carthage

Sophonisba let herself inside the great hall of the Barca compound and immediately sensed that something was not right. She went up to her quarters and found the servant girl snoozing off while rocking Didobal in her cradle. The baby slept peacefully. Sophonisba leaned over the cradle and felt her baby's soft, warm cheek. She kissed her baby curls.

The servant girl jerked awake. "I didn't hear you come in," she said.

"Is everything okay?" Sophonisba asked.

The girl nodded. She glanced down at the baby and back up at Sophonisba.

"Where's Lady Barca?" she asked.

The girl shrugged. She followed Sophonisba from the room and across the landing to Lady Barca's quarters.

"Lady Barca," Sophonisba called.

The rooms were empty. If she wasn't well enough to go to her daughter's wedding, then where could she possibly be? For Sophonisba, in place of all the anger she'd felt before opening the door to the Barca compound, now there was only dread.

She raced back to the landing and paused, considering where to look next.

A scream split the air right behind Sophonisba. She jumped and spun. The servant girl was looking up and pointing, horror fixed on her face as if she had turned to stone.

A hot fist grabbed Sophonisba's gut as she looked in the direction of the servant's gaze, up toward the rafters.

Lady Barca dangled by the neck from the rafters, a silk curtain tied around her neck.

Sophonisba heard a thump as the servant girl crumpled to the ground behind her, but she didn't take her eyes from Lady Barca's lifeless body. Shame and anguish cut to her core. For several minutes she didn't move, as one realization after another washed through her. She'd said so many hateful things to Lady Barca. *You're betraying your word. Death would be better,* Sophonisba had told her. But Lady Barca had always agreed.

Lady Barca had commanded them to carry through with the wedding knowing that she would not see it, knowing that she alone would carry the shame of her betrayal to her grave. In commanding her children to comply with her wishes, she had saved them from their portion of shame. In her death, she had preserved their honor.

Tears clouded her eyes, and she sank to her knees. As she wept, she dug her fingernails into her neck, realizing that here before her was the empty vessel of an honorable woman.

CHAPTER 57

Council Chamber, Carthage

Geromachus slipped into the dark, empty council chamber. In the space of three days, Sapanibal had married the pretender, Lady Barca had taken her own life, and Ida Hanna had persuaded the people to angry rioting. Even from inside the great city hall he could hear the sounds of rioters storming the streets to the Barca compound, ready to demand an end to the Roman war and prison for Hannibal Barca. Ida's plot to take over the city just might work, too, Geromachus thought. There was certainly nothing he could do anymore. Grief weighed on his heart. He'd already played all the cards in his hand and lost a dear friend in the process.

He shuffled further into the chamber and looked around. His old eyes weren't good in the dark anymore, and he barely made out the outline of the table.

"Ida? It's Geromachus," he said. Ida had asked to meet him here. He shouldn't have come so late at night. He was an old man. His peers were dead. His body was frail. There was little holding him to this life. If Ida wished to trap him here to kill him, then he was not afraid. Only men enamored with youth feared death. For Geromachus, youth was a long-dead dream.

Still, if there was a chance that Ida wanted to strike another compromise, then he should do what he could. If there
was a shred of honor left in Ida Hanna, then maybe Carthage
was not yet lost.

"Ida?" he called again, looking more deeply into the shadows.

A man streaked from the shadows, dagger glinting and
aimed for Geromachus's neck. "Your loyalty to the Barcas is
no longer appreciated," Ida Hanna's voice said.

Geromachus didn't fight. He took his last fleeting breath
before the dagger pierced his windpipe. Warm blood spurted, and pain thrust him to the floor, where he writhed in ag-
ony on the cold tiles. The pain swallowed what strength his
body had left.

So it was a trap. Then surely Carthage was doomed, not to
Rome, but to her own avarice.

Soon, his body was still.

CHAPTER 58

Barca Compound, Carthage

The gate to the Barca compound rattled. Shouts filled the courtyard. Pots and pans banged on the building's walls closest to the street and echoed through the house.

Sophonisba raced through the house, securing all the windows and doors. Hamilcar cried and clung to her robes, terrified of the screams.

"Double bar the doors!" she called to the servants. "Arm yourselves, and stand guard through the night. No one enters or exits this house." Adrenaline zipped through her body and made her hands shake. Was this how her husband felt at battle? No, she thought. Battle was his life. She imagined that he would be calm and focused. She took a slow breath in through her nose, drawing strength from Hannibal's courage.

She checked the front door herself, hearing the yells more distinctly from there. "Stop the war! Bankrupt Barca! Bankrupt Barca!"

The words chilled her. She had no more power to stop the war than they did. And what if she did? Hannibal would come home, and then what? Would Rome chase him to his doorstep and set the entire city aflame? She'd heard the stories of the last war with Rome. This war could end just as badly if they gave up too soon.

But she couldn't make them understand that, not when they were screaming down murderous threats on her family. There was no sense in an angry mob. *What would Lady Barca do right now?* she wondered. She would have said something strong and sensible, and Sophonisba wouldn't have felt so helpless. But she was helpless. She was completely alone now. Her husband and his brother were far away. Her mother-in-law was dead. Her sister-in-law was married off to an impostor. She wasn't a native of Carthage. There was nothing she could do. She felt truly alone.

As she shut the last open curtain, she caught a glimpse of Ida's satisfied smile. He encouraged the mob and joined with their chant. He had probably started the chant. Useless anger coursed through her, making her feel weak, like a bird trapped under a bear's paw.

Hamilcar wrapped his arms around her legs. "Momma," he cried. "Momma, I'm scared."

She leaned down, picked him up, and carried him upstairs to where Didobal cried in her cradle. Right now, the only thing she could do was comfort her children and pray that the gods would see fit to show mercy to her family.

She remembered Hannibal's prediction, the prophecy he'd seen in the stars so long ago, and wondered if the omen was not a warning of the war against Rome, but of Carthage's war against itself.

CHAPTER 59

Carthaginian Camp, Outside of Rome

Hannibal felt as though an arrow had pierced his gut. He had just heard the news of his city's betrayal of the true Numidian king and of his sister's sudden marriage to the new pretender. He was angry and confused about it. He had no idea how his mother could have let this happen. The note he'd received had no details, and the messenger had been unable to tell him anything further.

He heard Massinissa coming long before the man threw open his tent. Every pore of his face seethed. "Hannibal Barca, friend of Numidia," he said caustically.

Hannibal looked at the officers poring over maps and the Sacred Band Members standing ready to defend him. "Leave us," he said to all of them.

All but Maherabal rushed to do as Hannibal bid.

"You as well," Hannibal said.

Maherabal hesitated before following the other members of the Sacred Band from the tent, no doubt only to stand right outside the tent flap, ready to barge in the moment he sensed danger.

Hannibal sat, placing his palms down on the table with

the maps. "I received news of Scyla's betrayal," he said, hoping to head off Massinissa's accusations.

Massinissa ripped the maps from the tabletop and heaved them onto the floor. His eyes flamed and his hands shook.

Hannibal stood.

"Carthage, your city, has been the architect of my downfall," he said. "My mother has been murdered and my kingdom destroyed."

Hannibal winced. The bit of a note he had received had left out these details as well. He shook his head. "I didn't know. You must know I had nothing to do with it."

"It doesn't matter," Massinissa snapped. "We are not men tied to our swords. We require our kingdoms behind us."

A sinking feeling invaded Hannibal's stomach. An unexpected enemy strategy during battle he could handle, but this...he could not eliminate Scyla and put Numidia back together from here. He couldn't unmarry his sister from the pretender. He couldn't fix this, but he had to try. "We're in the midst of our final push toward Rome. When I return to Africa, I will make this right. My family and I will stand behind the true king of Numidia."

"Would you stand idly by while your house was used and plundered by a stranger?"

The answer hung in the air between them. *No.*

"But I can't stand idly by while my ally deserts me on the eve of victory against Rome," Hannibal said.

"Overnight you have become my enemy," Massinissa said, "by your own city's hand."

"Then all of our work has been for nothing. You would give that up?" For a long moment, neither of them spoke.

What had gone wrong back home? Hannibal didn't understand. His mother had always been able to hold her own against the Hannas. What had changed, and why was the Council suddenly eager to welcome this Scyla as the king of Numidia? All he had were guesses, and it made him want to explode with frustration.

"That's not my concern," Massinissa said.

Anger welled in Hannibal, and he leaped over the table and shoved Massinissa to the ground like a wild animal. He pinned him to the floor and drew his knife. "Enemies then." He slammed the knife down toward Massinissa's armor.

"Hannibal!" Massinissa shouted.

Hannibal stood and stepped back. Part of him wished he had the nerve to kill his former friend for this betrayal, but Massinissa had shown nothing but courage in battle, and none of this was his fault.

Massinissa looked down at the knife handle, engraved with the Barca family crest and surrounded in loops and curlicues carved into the metal. Instead of seeing his chest pooling with blood, he saw that the knife was stuck through the armor along his side. He pulled the knife free and sat up. "You could have killed me," he said.

"What good would that do? But if you leave now, you'll be killing me," Hannibal said.

Massinissa stood and brushed the dust from his armor in a few nervous swipes.

Hannibal looked into his former friend's eyes, sad for the loss of his friendship at least as much as he was sad for the loss of the Numidian cavalry in his march against Rome. "Please know I had nothing to do with this," Hannibal said.

Massinissa frowned but nodded once. "You wouldn't be so stupid."

The air in the tent hung heavy, and neither spoke for a long moment.

"Godspeed in your endeavors," Hannibal said. "May we meet again."

"Yes, brother," Massinissa said. He laid the knife on the edge of the table, turned, and strode from the tent. He was a proud man, but his steps showed weariness. He had a long road to walk before he would regain his kingdom, and Hannibal feared that his own road bore a striking resemblance.

He reached down and picked up the knife from the table. Running his thumb along the Barca family crest, he wondered what his father would have done in this situation.

He didn't know. Carthage had always backed Hamilcar Barca. The reality stung.

CHAPTER 60

Rome's City Walls

The Roman guard patrolling the walls fidgeted with the hilt of his sword as he walked the length of the wall. Hannibal was close. Too close. The guard had felt so confident in Rome's ability to keep the Carthaginian army out, and yet, here they were, two battles lost and the enemy marching freely in the countryside. Did the old men in the Senate not remember how to wage battle? Were they senile? What was the use of electing old consuls if they couldn't remember how to fight?

At least they had Scipio. Like everyone in Rome, the guard had heard all about Scipio's narrow escape from Hannibal's clutches. Scipio knew how to fight, but would the old dogs on the Senate listen to someone so young?

"Mars give us all strength," he said. Did Mars even hear a poor soldier with nothing but a long career of wall patrol field drills?

He turned on his heel to walk back in the opposite direction. Beyond him, slivers of blue smoke rose like pillars in the air. Every thought disappeared from his mind as he stopped walking. His shoulders turned rigid and his eyes narrowed. Tiny purple flags flapped over the camp. The soldier's eyes widened and lines creased his forehead. After years of guard duty and drills, he finally had a reason to send an alert. It both thrilled and terrified him.

He turned, cupped his hands around his mouth and shouted, "Hannibal at the gates! Hannibal at the gates!"

Below him, his words echoed off the rock walls and rippled through the crowded streets.

"Hannibal's at the gates!" the Romans cried.

They turned in circles like ants disrupted from their intended path, as if the pronouncement was the equivalent of the curse of death. Many of them raced toward the center of the city, shouting, "Hannibal at the gates!"

The cry ballooned throughout the city.

CHAPTER 61

The Roman Senate

The air inside the Senate chamber was dry and empty, devoid of the cries that reigned outside in the streets and courtyards. The eyes of the Roman Senate stayed with Scipio as he walked to the front of the room and stood before them. The old senators waited for his words, some with admiration in their faces and others with thinly veiled disdain, but none of them objected to his place at the front of the room.

Scipio breathed deeply of the tense air. He was right, and they knew it. They had to listen to him. Still, it unnerved him to know that some senators resented being told what to do by one so young, even if he had been the only one to guess Hannibal's plan, the only one to have met the man and lived.

"Hannibal may be at our gates, but he will come no further," Scipio said. "He is starved for reinforcements and can't conceivably occupy Rome with so few troops."

"The city is in panic," one of the senators said. "Hannibal must know that. He can use that to his advantage. We need to lure him away from the city before the streets of Rome become our worst enemy. What can we do if the citizens start rioting?"

Scipio held the senator's eyes for a moment and then let his gaze roam over the room. "I have raised eight legions of the finest men from every district. If we play our hand right, we can push Hannibal back for good. If we lose these men, we deserve to forfeit the city."

"What's your proposal?" another senator asked.

Scipio lifted his chin. "I have left four legions in camp outside of the city in the care of Varro and Paulus. They will signal their presence to Hannibal, and he will be forced to follow them west into battle. Away from the city walls."

"And you?" said one of the most skeptical old senators.

Scipio held the old man's stare, refusing to blink. "I will use Hannibal's strategy against him. The remaining four legions will accompany me to the shores of Africa. I have struck an alliance with the deposed king of Numidia. With his help, we will press down on Carthage, effecting Hannibal's immediate return to defend his home."

Scipio didn't wait for the senators to respond. He strode toward the door ahead of him, not pausing to give them room to discuss this with him. As he stepped over the threshold, he unclenched his fists. For the good of Rome, the Senate would back him on this. They had to know that it was their refusal to heed his previous advice that had lodged them between Hannibal's army and a rioting city.

This time would be different. He could feel it.

CHAPTER 62

Cartagena

Hasdrubal stood at the window of his office in Cartagena. Every day since Hannibal had left, he'd paced in front of it, hoping to receive marching orders from his brother. Hannibal had said not to leave Carthage undefended. Hannibal couldn't know that Carthage had turned on herself and taken their own mother as a casualty. It was too late.

The rain, while formerly an annoyance, threatened to drown him in melancholy, and the food here tasted blander than ever. He would almost give up any hope of seeing a real battle just for some red chili in his dinner. Even the women here had ceased to be interesting to him.

He'd waited, hoping for some word, but his grief needed a distraction. He had to act.

A knock sounded at the door, and he opened it. The scribe entered. Droplets of mist clung to his cloak. Did it ever stop raining here?

"You sent for me?" the scribe said.

Hasdrubal ignored the obvious statement and gestured for the scribe to sit.

The young man took out a piece of parchment, prepared

his pen, and waited for Hasdrubal to speak.

Hannibal wasn't going to like hearing from him again. He'd say to stay. Wouldn't he? But if Carthage was lost to Ida Hanna, what could be the purpose of sticking around? It was time that he carried the Barca name himself. He was done asking for his brother's permission.

"All is lost in Carthage, brother," Hasdrubal said. "I come to your aid in Italy. I will follow your path across the Alps and join you in Umbria."

Silence hovered in the room for a long moment as the scribe worked to compose his features into a disinterested mask. Hasdrubal debated how much more he should say. Maybe he'd already put too much in the note. There was always the possibility of interception.

"That's it," he said to the scribe, who folded the parchment and sealed the letter.

CHAPTER 63

En Route, the Alps

The letter traversed the Iberian Peninsula, the Pyrenees, and Gaul, belted to the messenger's waist. Near the top of the Alps, the messenger's horse trotted through the snow, slipped, and slowed to a walk. The messenger prodded the weary horse on.

"It's all downhill from here, buddy," he said to his horse. His voice shook in the brittle cold. He knew that going down the mountains was every bit as treacherous as going up them. He set his jaw and urged the horse to move faster.

CHAPTER 64

En Route, Northern Italian Countryside

The messenger blinked hard several times in a row. It was hard to tell if the night was empty and black or if his eyes were too weary to see anything but the blurred outline of grass waving against his horse's legs. He should have made camp and gotten a few winks of sleep, but he was so close. At least, he thought he was. The snow was gone, and it had been how many days since he'd left the foothills in northern Italy? He tried to think, but he couldn't focus his memory.

Every time he drifted to sleep he dreamed that he was arriving in the foothills of the Alps or prodding his numb horse through the sudden snowstorm on his way down the mountain or arriving at the banks of the Tiber River, drinking and drinking, unable to quench his thirst. Reality melded with his dreams until he couldn't tell the difference. He tried to swallow the cool water that filled his hands but only felt air hitting the back of his parched throat.

Something cracked in the night nearby. He jerked on the horse's back, the vision of the river fading away. It sounded like a stick snapping. From under the horse's feet? Who would follow him so late at night? Was it late? It must be.

He drifted again, this time seeing the gates of Rome before him. Were they glowing or was that the sunshine reflecting off the shiny stones? He was so close. He just needed to follow the wall until it led him to General Hannibal. He just had to find the General. He circled the wall again and again.

Something smacked him in the face, and he felt himself falling from the horse's back. As he fell, he noticed that it was dark, and the city walls were nowhere in sight. He wasn't near Rome at all.

As a tingling pain spread across his face, he put out his arm to break his fall and felt it give under him as the weight of his entire body fell on it. The corresponding crack vibrated into his shoulder right before the pain crashed through him.

Stars speckled his vision and heat burned inside his ears. What happened? Had he run into a tree branch while riding? He inhaled and the pain in his arm and face throbbed harder and hotter, making him feel like he was still falling.

As the messenger sank into oblivion, a shadow moved in the treetops along the path the horse and rider had been following. The figure dropped to the ground and crept over to the still form in the road. The man felt along the messenger's body until his fingers brushed the folded parchment and then pulled it from the belt.

He struck a bit of flint. The small ember of light danced against his red tunic as he opened the parchment and read the contents. Now Rome would know all.

CHAPTER 65

Northern Italian Countryside

Hasdrubal led his troops into a valley surrounded on all sides by sharp ridges, the last vestiges of the mountains they had just descended into northern Italy. The trek over the Alps had been difficult. No doubt they would be remembered less for coming second, after the Great Hannibal Barca. His men were due for a rest before making the final leg of the journey to Rome.

"No word from Hannibal yet?" Hasdrubal asked his captain.

The captain pressed his lips together and shook his head.

Worry gnawed at Hasdrubal, but he pushed it down. He had led his troops through the worst of it. He would simply have to meet Hannibal in Rome and hope that he wasn't too late getting there.

"We'll find him in Rome," Hasdrubal said, infusing his words with all the confidence he wanted to feel.

The captain nodded, "Yes, sir," though something in the way his eyes darted to the left and back up to Hasdrubal made Hasdrubal more nervous. A taut silence followed.

The captain finally broke the silence. "By my count, we've

passed through the Alps with considerably fewer losses than your brother had."

At this Hasdrubal had to smile. "He'll hate me for that."

He had spent weeks leading his thirty thousand troops through the icy mountains, and it sure beat sitting in his office in Cartagena doing nothing, waiting for Hannibal to decide to need him. He should have come sooner. The fresh air made him feel more alive than ever, like he could take on anything the elements threw at him. He would meet Hannibal in Rome, and together they would take the city. He knew they would.

The sound of a trumpet pierced the murmurs of his troops, who scrambled to circle up in the valley and build camps. The late afternoon sun shone from over the western ridge, at first disguising the sound's origin.

But then Hasdrubal saw it.

His stomach turned cold.

Legions of Roman soldiers poured over the ridges from the west, from the south, from the east, surrounding the worn out Carthaginian army. Their presence could only signify one thing; the Romans had intercepted Hasdrubal's message, which meant that Hannibal had no idea he was coming.

Hasdrubal breathed past the fist of fear that clenched in his chest. He could defeat these Romans. He had to. His army was large.

But he saw with a single sweeping glance around him that the Roman army was just as large, and probably larger. And they hadn't just finished traveling over the most treacherous mountain pass in the world.

"Circle round!" Hasdrubal called out to his men, trying to

shove down the panic that burned his chest. It was the same feeling he'd had staring into the face of the pouncing lion as a young boy. But this time, he couldn't freeze. Hannibal wasn't going to rescue him. He was a man now, he reminded himself. He didn't need his big brother to rescue him like a child. "Line up! Take your positions!" he shouted out, with more strength this time.

His men pulled up their camps and reached for their weapons. Panic flew through the air like a mist from the gods, landing on even the strongest. Hasdrubal kept barking orders. "Fall into rank! Circle around!"

But few men responded. He kicked his horse into motion, weaving his way through the men, shouting at them. How was it that Hannibal could inspire his troops with a single command, and Hasdrubal's troops balked in panic and refused to hear him? But these men weren't the battle-hardened men Hannibal had brought with him. Many of these men were barely more than boys who had never tasted battle before, and their eagerness for war had died as soon as they saw the Romans barreling down the mountain ridges toward them.

"Circle round!" Hasdrubal called out.

A few men came to attention and stepped in line with him, but he sensed that most of his men could think only of survival.

The Roman horn blasted again, this time louder.

"Defend yourselves, men!" Hasdrubal shouted. "Come with me, all who would die fighting Rome!" He pivoted his horse to face the oncoming Romans, turning his back on his fear. It was time to stop thinking and do.

"Lions of Carthage!" he shouted. He kicked his horse savagely and charged at the Romans, sword ready to slay Roman flesh.

A few soldiers followed their fearless leader and disappeared through the Roman front lines. The Romans circled the Carthaginians, swallowing them like a spoonful of broth.

CHAPTER 66

215 BCE, Camp Outside of Rome

Hannibal paced the length of his tent. Sweat shone on his face, mirroring the moisture that he refused to let fall from his eyes. Word had just arrived from Sophonisba.

The messenger waited quietly near the entrance to the tent, the parchment flapping between his hands as though it, too, was reeling from its contents.

Maherabal sat in the corner, grave and waiting.

Hannibal turned and faced him. "Send a detachment immediately to Hasdrubal in Iberia. Tell him to march back to Africa and put Carthage under martial law."

Maherabal's eyebrows rose incrementally. "General, you are not a dictator," he said quietly.

"I'm not a fool, either," Hannibal said.

Maherabal's face didn't change.

Hannibal continued. "My house is rife with the stench of my mother's corpse. My sister is raped by the pretender to the Numidian throne. My wife is besieged by Ida Hanna's henchmen. What of Carthage?" His voice rose with each statement.

Maherabal stood and met his gaze, his jaw set. "I swear on my life every traitor will die slowly at the end of a torturer's knife." He paused. "But don't act on vengeance alone."

The simmering rage that filled Hannibal's entire being ignited at Maherabal's words. He drew his sword and deftly swung it at Maherabal's neck, stopping the blade a hair's width from his flesh.

Maherabal didn't flinch.

"Vengeance alone!" Hannibal shouted. "What do you think this whole war is about? All I have is vengeance!"

He swung from the other side, again stopping the blade a hair's width from Maherabal's neck.

Again, Maherabal didn't flinch. He didn't draw his own blade, but instead stared Hannibal in the face with calm eyes. "Carthage is not Rome," Maherabal said. He held Hannibal's eyes.

Like he'd been drenched with icy water, Hannibal's rage sizzled out. He lowered his sword. Carthage *was* no Rome. Carthage was the home he loved and fought for. Even now, when his city had betrayed him, he couldn't stop fighting for her. He thought of his poor mother, of Sophonisba and his small children. He remembered the sign he'd seen in the stars so many fortnights ago. The gods hadn't misled him after all. But maybe there was still hope.

He turned to the messenger, who still waited near the entrance to the tent. "Send an armed detachment to my brother in Cartagena. Tell him to return to Carthage to stand for the Barcas at council."

The messenger nodded and left.

Hannibal felt Maherabal's capable hand on his shoulder.

"I won't rest until this has all been put right," Maherabal said.

Hannibal nodded. He could still win this war. He had to. He had come too far not to. Leaving meant defeat. Hasdrubal might still win Carthage's loyalty back. He was charming, and people liked him.

"General! Come quickly!" one of the captains called from outside the tent.

Hannibal's pulse spiked. He strode from the tent with Maherabal at his heels.

Outside, the captain motioned for Hannibal to follow, and the three men walked through the camp toward the fortifications.

"The scouts have just reported seeing four Roman legions west of us at the fields of Cannae," the captain said.

"And in Rome?" Hannibal asked.

"Scipio's legions are still there. A direct attack is not a good idea without reinforcements."

Hannibal glanced over at Maherabal. "Mobilize camp. We march for Cannae at once."

"We've marched an army to the gates of Rome and now we turn back?" Maherabal pointed out.

Hannibal drew his eyebrows down and felt the hilt of his sword. "Roman power isn't inside those city walls. Win over the countryside, her allies, and she will crumble like the corrupt, diseased politician that she is."

"A Roman horseman approaches!" a guard from atop the fortifications shouted.

Hannibal looked between the cracks in the makeshift camp wall protecting the camp and beyond to where the guard pointed.

A lone rider galloped closer with something dangling

from his left hand. With each stride the horse took, the item flopped against the horse's belly. The rider paused outside the fortification, but instead of requesting an audience, the rider stopped thirty paces away and flung the object from the bottom of the saddle in a wide arching motion over his head.

It soared over the camp wall.

Hannibal turned to watch it appear on his side of the fortification. Damp dirt thudded under the item not three paces from Hannibal's feet as it rolled and stopped. Hannibal strode over to get a better look, kicking it over. A severed head? What could this possibly mean?

The head rolled over in the dirt and Hasdrubal's once handsome face stared blankly up at Hannibal, his chiseled jaw nothing more than a dirt mush. His brother's head, caked in blood and lying in the mud at his feet. Eyes grayed and blank, crusted with flies. Always the handsome one of the brothers, he'd lost his beauty. He'd also lost his fear, his need for approval. In death, Hasdrubal was finally free.

Shock froze his legs and seared his chest. Rage turned his face hot, then cold, then hot again. The scream of an enraged animal lit the air. First his city, then his mother, then his brother? What more could Rome take from him? Hasdrubal was dead. Hannibal couldn't save him. They weren't children. This was war. Grief and anger struggled inside him. He looked over at Maherabal, whose face reflected the horror and fury he felt inside.

Rome wanted war. Hannibal would give them hell.

"To Cannae!"

He ripped a spear from a nearby guard's hand and raced to the camp's front gate. He lowered his shoulder as he hit the wooden gate, forcing it open. He set his feet, aimed with rapid precision, and launched the spear at the escaping Roman.

The spear arched fast and high into the air. The blade glinted in the sun and then dropped. It hit its mark in the back, gliding effortlessly through the man's armor, body, and horse, driving them both into the dirt with a satisfying thud.

Hannibal grabbed the nearest horse, swung himself on top of it, and kicked it to a canter. "To Cannae!" he shouted. "Kill those Roman bastards!"

Shouts echoed from around the camp, swarming closer as his men tore down the camp and picked up their weapons in mere minutes.

"To Cannae to get those bastards!" The men around him repeated the words until they melted into a stream of unintelligible shouts from the voices joining as one.

The Sacred Band thundered behind him.

CHAPTER 67

Cannae

Hannibal hit the fields of Cannae at a sprint and pulled his horse up at the sight of the Roman legions camped across the way. Fury and adrenaline flooded his veins, making him want to ride into the Roman camp and single-handedly defeat the entire army, but reason won out over the reckless rage. He pulled his horse up and watched his army form ranks behind him. Rushing in would bring certain defeat.

He inhaled and let his breath out slowly. The cloud of dust from his horse's feet blew up and billowed north, toward the Romans. The sun beat against the back of his head, an ally today, as the Romans would be forced to fight squinting into the sun. Had they not considered this when selecting the field of battle? At times, Hannibal felt blessed with an incompetent enemy.

His cavalry was split in half, flanking the center line on either side. The Libyan infantry was stacked twenty deep on the left, and the Iberian and Celtic infantry mirrored the Libyans on the right. The Carthaginian veterans linked the two flanks in the center only three deep. It was thin but sufficient for Hannibal's plan.

Minerix rode up beside him. "My men are in line. Are you sure about this arrangement?"

"Yes," Hannibal said.

The two studied the Roman army as it assembled across the field in a phalanx. There were thirty maniples command-ed by centurions, staggered three deep and packed elbow to elbow.

"Damn Romans are going to trip over each other," Min-erix said.

Hannibal smirked. "Works for us."

The Roman phalanx was flanked on both sides by cavalry. Every few minutes, consular guards rode out from behind the phalanx and then cut back behind the ranks, keeping an eye on Hannibal's army.

Hannibal urged his horse to walk once more, and Minerix kept pace with him.

"Even if they trip over each other and fall on their swords, they will win by sheer numbers," Minerix said. "And with your center line open like it is…"

"They won't win," Hannibal said.

"I'd like to believe you, son," Minerix said.

Hannibal glanced over at the Celtic chieftain and caught the paternal look in his eye. They'd become colleagues, but more than that, Hannibal had come to respect him. Some-thing about the strong set of jaw and stalwart nature remind-ed Hannibal of his own father.

Hannibal breathed slowly in through his nose. He'd given up his usual strategic advantages in order to force a quick battle, but this would work. He knew it would. His hands itched to slay Romans.

Maherabal rode up to them. His somber face gave nothing away. "The men are nearly in position, and I've readied your position."

Minerix squinted at the troops assembling behind them.

"You doubt me," Hannibal said to Minerix.

"This is the first battle you seem not to have thought through to the end," Minerix said. He held Hannibal's eyes.

Hannibal didn't flinch. He squeezed his fists tightly and narrowed his eyes. "I have thought this through, and it's the only way we're going to win. Do you remember the battle of Marathon? On that field, the Greeks had accidentally maneuvered the Persian advance into a collapsing pocket and then outflanked Xerxes on both sides. It was a blood bath."

Maherabal nodded. "We are the Greeks, I hope."

"But you're leaving the middle weak and yourself vulnerable," Minerix said.

"The Romans would like nothing more than to kill me," Hannibal said. "I dare them to try."

Minerix's eyes widened with understanding. "You're using yourself as bait."

Hannibal nodded.

"We just might win," Minerix said. He kicked his horse forward and trotted away to join his men.

Hannibal spun his horse to face his veterans.

They all looked at him, tensed and waiting for his instruction.

"Men, I've never asked the impossible from you," he said. "But I do today. You must hold the center line no matter what. There are more of them, and they will direct their greatest force on you in order to reach me."

A few of the men shifted, but they held their posture.

"If you hold the line," Hannibal continued, "we will win the day."

They stood still with their eyes on him, not optimistic, but not flinching from their duty.

Across the field, the Roman battle standards rose, waving in the wind, and the army charged forward toward the Carthaginian line.

Minerix raced off to join his men.

"Hold the line and we will win," Hannibal shouted, as the Romans screamed behind him. He rode to his place behind them and dismounted. Fifty spears surrounded him, planted in the ground like a cage. They were his artillery.

Maherabal dismounted beside Hannibal and joined him in the circle of spears. "The future of Carthage is in your hands," he said. "I'll stand with you to the end."

The growing thunder of Roman footsteps was only seconds away.

Hannibal unstuck the first spear from the ground and hurled it over the heads of his center line.

The spear hit its mark at the Roman center, crashing through a maniple's tortoise shell formation and skewering two Roman legionnaires.

Hannibal jerked the next spear free and aimed, sending it again into the Roman center, further crumbling it, just as he had planned.

Hannibal heard a shout go up from his men, and they whooped as the now-disorganized Roman front crashed into the Carthaginian weapons and went down one after another. A palpable shift of energy lit new vigor in Hannibal's army as they countered. Their longer swords slashed one Roman after another.

"Cavalry charge!" Maherabal shouted.

"Now!" Hannibal shouted. He jerked his last spear from the ground and fell sideways as his center line stretched thin in the center and retreated backwards to form the pocket. "Trap the bastards!"

The men around him shouted.

Both flanks of Carthaginian cavalry thundered forward. Carthage's left flank collided with Rome's Patrician cavalry, all rich sots more concerned with looking privileged than with their combat skills. The inexperienced young noblemen fell one after another under the hacking blows of the Carthaginians. The larger Iberian horses pushed the rest of the Patricians back until many of them turned their horses rabidly and fled in a futile attempt to avoid having their arms and heads severed and their intestines ripped to shreds around them.

At Carthage's right flank, the battle raged more ambiguously. The Latin cavalry held its own against Carthage's right flank, with neither side seeming to gain any ground.

The Roman center, while weakened, held firm, surging forward toward Hannibal and pushing his center line back further and further.

CHAPTER 68

Cannae

Minerix swung his huge battle ax again and again, cleaving Roman legionnaires in two. His men barreled into the bloody wake of his ax, felling Romans like foothill saplings. The Romans might as well have been trees waving their arms.

Minerix swung again. The Roman in the blade's path threw up his arms and screamed. The blade sliced the arms and head from his shoulders.

Minerix sensed the Romans filling the void where the Carthaginian center line had been minutes before, and the Libyan infantry surged to head them off. It was time for the big push.

"Turn them to the inside no matter the cost," Minerix shouted to his men, who had linked up with the Libyans to deliver the final blow. "All Rome is under your boot!"

The sight of their chief, swinging his ax like a man possessed and cutting Romans apart by the handful, ignited Celtic fury. With each step forward, he slashed down more and more soldiers.

Just as quickly, new Romans took their place. They surrounded Minerix, trying to cut him off from his troops.

"To the inside!" Minerix shouted. He caught a glimpse of his son, Kelin, shoving through the Romans.

"Father!" Kelin raised his ax high. He smashed it through the top of an enemy's head. The Roman staggered sideways. His sword, originally aimed at Minerix's side, grazed his elbow before slicing into another Roman's thigh.

Was Kelin's hand missing fingers? Minerix swung again. So much blood. His son's blood. His blood.

Kill the Romans. Kill them all. Kill. Kill. The words thrummed in Minerix's head. He saw nothing but necks to split. He shoved ahead, through rows of Romans, swinging his ax widely and then turning, forcing the Roman's to either try to stab him or back up further into Hannibal's trap.

Kill. Kill. Kill.

His men spread around him, forcing their way through the Roman lines.

Kill.

The Romans pushed into him, crowding around him.

Where were his men? They'd spread too thin. Had he gone too far into the Roman line? How many were dead? Kelin? He didn't dare scan the crowd. His men would catch up to him. He would blaze the trail. To lose focus was to lose a life.

He swung until the Romans crowded him too much. He couldn't bring his arm back far enough to leverage his ax. He launched his weapon into a centurion's chest.

The centurion fell, bringing several Romans with him.

Now weaponless but for his bare hands, Minerix leaped

onto a Roman legionnaire's head, pressing his thumbs into his eyes and gauging them out.

More Romans surrounded him, pricking him with their short swords like he was a pincushion.

Furious and fueled by wrath, he grabbed the nearest Roman and tore his arm out of his socket. He waved the disembodied arm through the air and slammed it down on a Roman's head. Blood sprayed armor. He beat the arm against a Roman's head until the man fell over. He rammed the arm to a bloody pulp and flung it over the sea of Romans. He reached for more Roman arms, ripping them free from bodies like ticks on a horse's back. He relished the horror in his enemies' eyes. Some turned away from him rather than see their countryman's severed hand beat them senseless.

Minerix caught a glimpse of his son, grappling a sword out of his opponent's grasp and using it to stab the man through the heart. A surge of fatherly pride added power to his own strokes.

Sizzling pain descended his spine. He was falling.

Celtic yells split the air. His men broke ranks. A hand reached to steady him as he fell.

He couldn't fall. Falling was death. His legs. He shouldn't feel them. He felt the cutting pain in his spinal column. He reached behind him as he fell. A sword was lodged in his back. His body weight brought down another handful of Romans. This was where it ended for him. This was the end. He wasn't ready. His son. His men. A guttural yell ripped from his throat.

His men roared with savage hatred as they watched their chief fall to his death. They fought harder and faster, pushing the Roman ranks toward the inside.

CHAPTER 69

Cannae

Hannibal heard the Celtic roar from across the field. A shiver ran through him. Minerix or Kelin. One of them had fallen. He grabbed a fallen spear from the ground beside him and whipped it forward. He could almost hear its whistle as it cut the air. The point skewered four Romans. They dropped to the ground.

The Carthaginian cavalry had circled around to join with the Libyan infantry, allowing the Roman flanks to fold together. The plan was working, but so much could still go wrong, and maybe already had.

The Carthaginian center line bulged backward to let the Romans fill in. The Romans, believing that the center line was retreating, shouted and fought with renewed vigor.

But the center line wasn't defeated. Hannibal's men stopped backing up when they were in line with Hannibal. This was a planned retreat. A trap of inches and angles.

"Hold them tight!" Hannibal shouted.

They held their ground. The Romans were entirely surrounded.

Hannibal grabbed another spear of the ground and

launched it. It was time. "Elephants, now!" he shouted.

A dozen war elephants charged forward from the grove of trees bordering the Carthaginian camp. They trumpeted. A few tried to turn around, frightened by the battle noises.

"Make holes!" Hannibal shouted.

His men responded instantly, moving laterally to make paths just big enough for the elephants to charge through. Their giant ears flapped. Several archers clung to the sides of the Mahout harnesses, using their positions in midair to rapidly pick off Romans. Trunks bigger and stronger than grown men swung back and forth. One man was hit and stumbled to the ground. He dragged himself desperately across the ground to avoid another hit. More men ducked to avoid being struck, and elephants tunneled through the ranks.

The elephants would prove to be the game changer. They terrified and obliterated the Roman ranks. The beasts crashed into the Roman line. The Romans shouted, trying to withdraw, but the Carthaginian army had them surrounded.

As if the panic surrounding them was fuel, the elephants whipped their trunks more furiously. They rose on their hind feet, crushing down on the Roman ranks. Flattened bodies piled in their wake. The Roman ranks were shattered. There would be no regrouping. They tried to run but bumped into one another. Their last choice was between falling by Carthaginian swords or beneath the trampling elephant.

"No prisoners!" Hannibal shouted. He grabbed a final spear. He jammed the tip into the ground out in front of him. Gripping the end with his right hand, he raced forward, flexing his quads. He leaped into the air, using the spear to catapult himself over the heads of his men in front of him. He let go of the spear midair and whipped two swords from his armor behind him. He landed in the middle of the Roman legion, knees bent, swords aimed at two Roman necks.

He swiftly brought both swords around at once, sending their heads tumbling from their necks. Hannibal slowly rose to his full height as the Roman bodies collapsed like falling trees. His eyes scanned the crowd of red cloaks. Who would challenge a Barca?

Roman soldiers looked to each other, hoping someone else would step up to take on the mighty Hannibal. Their hesitation was Hannibal's cue. He plowed forward and hacked through them like a scythe through the grain.

A blanket of dead Romans littered the battleground. Hannibal knew that his own losses had to be nearly as devastating. He watched one of his men grapple with a Roman soldier who had gone wild with panic. The two swords clashed bitterly, held for a moment, and then the Roman sword slipped forward, shoving into the Carthaginian soldier's abdomen.

Hannibal ran forward, sword extended, shoving his sword into the Roman's spine. He was winning. His strategy was working perfectly, but it was costing him dearly. He looked out over the field and saw one of the Roman generals riding from the field, followed closely by his flowing red cape and his guards. He held his sword uselessly in his right hand as he dodged several Carthaginians.

Fucking coward, Hannibal thought. They killed his brother and then refused to even send worthy adversaries to battle. His stomach burned and his temples pounded. This general would die. He reached down and ripped a spear from a fallen Libyan soldier's stomach. Then, he took careful aim and hurled it at the general's back.

The spear ran clean through the general and ended in one of his guards. The Roman general slumped down, screaming. His scream halted as he fell from his horse, dragging his guard with him.

Death was too gracious for these cowards.

CHAPTER 70

Cannae

General Paulus heard General Varro's chest-splitting scream and watched him fall backward off his horse. Every other sound dropped away from his consciousness but for that scream.

He remembered the night, several moons ago, when they'd both sat in the crowded Senate hall, waiting for the election results to come in for the two consulate positions that were voted on every two years. Being one of Rome's two consuls was the highest ruling position in Rome. Paulus had already served one two-year term, and he'd decided to run again. He had every intention of making it his personal mission to starve out Hannibal Barca and rid Rome of the pestilence. His plan was the best of everyone running for the consulate. He knew that Hannibal didn't have many supplies left, and rumor had it that Carthage was refusing to support her general. Rome had only to cut off any supply routes, and victory was theirs without shedding a drop of Roman blood.

The murmurs in the hall had quieted as an elderly senator walked down the center aisle to the front of the room to read the votes. He cleared his throat and looked down at the parchment in his hands. "The elected consuls for the next two years are Lucius Aemilius Paulus and Gaius Terentius Varro."

Paulus's eyes met Varro's from across the room. They'd never been friends—more like brothers who disagreed on everything—but in that golden moment, they formed an un-breakable bond. Together they would rule Rome. Together they'd vanquish Hannibal from Rome's doorstep. Varro was a man of action, but how could he fail to see the sense of Paulus's plan? They both stood to thundering applause.

But that first moment was the only moment of unity the two experienced. Varro hadn't seen the sense of Paulus's simple plan.

"Where is the glory in starving him to death?" Varro said. "Are you a coward afraid to face battle? We could be rid of Hannibal now, and you want to drag it on through the winter?"

So the two consuls had taken turns leading the troops. When it was Paulus's turn, he sent men to the harbors and roads to block supply routes. When it was Varro's turn, those troops were brought back to march closer to Hannibal's camp.

And it had brought them here. To Cannae. To a field oozing with Roman blood and carnage.

Paulus rode hard to Varro's side, hoping against hope that the man was alive. Why hadn't Varro understood that forcing an open battle would come to this? He was going to die. There was no way around it, and Paulus was sorry. They were countrymen, brothers, and this was a horrible way to die.

He arrived next to Varro in time to watch blood gurgle

from his mouth. Varro's chest spasmed as he tried to speak.

"I was wrong," Varro said. He choked on his words, and his eyes rolled backward in his skull.

Paulus dismounted and slapped Varro cheek. "No. You can't die," he said. "You wanted this. This was your idea." Anger filled him.

Varro's body gave a final spasm and then was still.

Paulus put his hand over Varro's mouth, but there was no breath.

He stood and jerked himself back on his horse. Looking around, he saw his disintegrating army surrounded by Africans and the General Hannibal himself taking aim with another spear.

Madness flooded Paulus, like none he'd ever experienced before. This hadn't been his idea. It wasn't fair. He didn't want this battle, and yet, here he was, about to die. But he wasn't going to die before he killed Hannibal Barca. He would die with honor.

"Hannibal!" he shrieked.

With a shout of denial, Paulus kicked his horse forward. He heard the remaining members of his Consular Guard follow him in hot pursuit. He whipped his sword from its sheath, ready to attack.

CHAPTER 71

Cannae

Hannibal again grabbed his dual swords from the ground after launching spears at the Roman officers. The second general met Hannibal's eyes, and Hannibal knew that the man intended to slaughter him or die trying.

He'll die trying, Hannibal thought. He braced himself and positioned his swords to swing the second the general came within range.

As the general bore down on horseback, Hannibal made a swift calculation and then swung, slicing the horse's front legs off.

The horse reeled forward.

Hannibal leaped back, avoiding the beast's heavy weight and the general's pointed sword.

The general slid forward until he was at Hannibal's shoulder height.

He slammed his right-hand sword down from his left shoulder and into the general's back.

The general, unable to stop himself, pitched forward, glancing off of Hannibal's shoulder. Hannibal shoved the dead weight to the ground and looked up to see a dozen consular guards spitting and swinging for his throat.

Hannibal ducked and rolled, deflecting one and the next and stabbing a third in the groin. He wrenched his left hand up and grazed another, but they parried in time to avoid a fatal blow. As quickly as they retreated, they returned full force. Hannibal's mind flipped ahead, planning out each move with rapid succession.

One of the guards grazed his shoulder. Another got his shin.

No matter how many moves ahead Hannibal could think, there was no way he could outthink the brawn of a dozen trained Roman guards.

He took a staggering hit to the chest. It didn't break his armor, but it set him off balance. He took another hit to the armor. And another. Blood streamed onto his hands. His own blood.

Hannibal dodged a nearly fatal blow and jumped to the opposite side, falling to the ground and rolling backward in an attempt to stall for a quick second or two.

As he jumped to his feet once again, Maherabal leaped in front of him, deflecting four men with one hand and another three with his other, allowing Hannibal to fully inhale.

"Took you long enough!" he said.

"Aye, General," Maherabal said, sticking a guard in the stomach.

Hannibal turned so that his back was to Maherabal's, and they fought off the Roman guards back to back.

But by now it wasn't just the Roman guards. Roman soldiers had joined them, and Hannibal and Maherabal swung harder and faster to vanquish them, two by two.

Adrenaline spiked down Hannibal's spine. His mind was emptied of everything but his next few moves, and though he bled, he didn't feel pain. The gods were giving him the strength he needed for one moment at a time.

Hannibal saw a break in the lines of Romans. The dark faces of his own countrymen, gleaming with sweat, appeared in front of him and cut down the last of the Roman guard. With the Roman guard demolished, the rank-and-file Roman soldiers took a few more poorly aimed slashes.

The Carthaginian forces now completely surrounded what was left of the Roman army. They backed up, running into the Carthaginian infantry. The moment they noticed that all was lost, they dropped their weapons.

"Mercy!" a Roman shouted.

The others joined him.

Hannibal stepped closer. His army followed him.

The Romans' cries for mercy became wails. The cowardly shrieks lit the air. "No, no, NO, NOOO!"

Hannibal plunged his sword one final time into a Roman chest. The scream stuck in the Roman's throat, turning to a bloody gargle in the back of his throat. As Hannibal removed his weapon, the Roman fell backwards onto the heap of his dead countrymen.

Maherabal sheathed one of his swords. "You're bleeding," he said to Hannibal. He put his now free arm around Hannibal's shoulder.

Hannibal looked down at the gash in his shin. It should hurt. It would later. He looked up at the men standing before him. He thrust his sword in the air. "Lions of Carthage."

Maherabal helped Hannibal across the battlefield, where

thousands of bodies already began to rot in the heat of the sinking sun, evidence of how expensive the battle had been.

Hannibal wondered if it had only been a day or if they had fought for several. Now that it was over, he found that his mind was weak from fatigue and the details blurred together. Had it been dark? Had they fought for many days and nights in a row? Maybe. He couldn't remember.

Hannibal wondered if Maherabal was holding him up or if he was holding up Maherabal. But it didn't matter. The battle was done.

Carthage had won.

CHAPTER 72

Cannae Camp

Stars glowed in the black sky. Some of them hung low like candles on the quiet field. They seemed to shift slightly with each passing minute, and so did Hannibal's faith in his homeland and in himself. His chest burned, hungry to be back in battle, killing Romans.

The whole camp was silent. Even the crickets were too tired to chirp. Gazing back up to the stars, he saw that not even the gods were saying anything.

Hannibal sat by what was left of his campfire. Only embers glowed in the slight breeze, and he shivered under the fur that covered his back. His fingers fidgeted with a blood-soaked figurine of a Roman soldier, turning it around slowly against his palm.

Every muscle in his body was stiff and sore. He'd sewed up the deep gash in his leg himself and dressed the throbbing wound in his shoulder. The injuries were a reminder of his victory but also of the heavy losses his army had suffered. He knew that, although there were still Romans out there to kill, he wouldn't be able to win another battle like that again.

Maherabal opened his eyes from across the fire pit.

Though Hannibal didn't look at him, he could feel Maherabal's eyes on him.

"What are the stars telling you tonight?" Maherabal asked.

Hannibal kept his eyes on the sky.

"They haven't changed," Hannibal said.

"So then you know our fate. You read it from the sky like you read a message on parchment."

"Men choose their own fate," Hannibal said. The words came out harder than he meant them to sound. He paused. *Did* men choose their own fate, or was that simply something he wanted to believe? What choices did he have if his fate was already sealed? "But the fate of empires is decided on another plane. The stars are the same."

Maherabal shifted his weight. "The night after our great victory and you are the only one without need for sleep," he said, his tone artificially light.

"My needs will not be met with sleep," Hannibal said. "The fire burns too deeply, my friend."

"Inside every soldier burns a fire."

Hannibal knew Maherabal was trying to help, but his spirit refused to be bolstered. "This is not a soldier's fire."

"We all hate Rome," Maherabal said.

"No man hates like a Barca hates, and I've lost control of it. It consumes me. It blots away love, drowns out fear. It has become my honor."

"You are the most honorable man of Carthage," Maherabal said.

"Then Carthage is lost."

"Is that what you've read in the stars tonight?"

"No."

"Then it is your choice."

Hannibal looked away from the stars and threw the figurine into the embers. Flames grew up around the figure, consuming it slowly until it was just another ember burning in the fire.

"There is no choice," he said. His words settled over him. With all the hate in his heart, it wouldn't matter. There was only one honorable path he could take, and he was on it. He knew it. Maherbal knew it. Every battle hardened, Rome-hating veteran in his army knew it.

All at once, fatigue fogged his mind. Today there had been victory, but it would only get harder from here. He wondered how many more battles there were and how many more of his men would have to die. He lay down on his mat, and sleep blanketed him almost instantly.

CHAPTER 73

Brindisi Harbor, Southern Italy

Scipio and Massinissa sat on horseback high above the Brindisi harbor, watching thousands of soldiers loading onto galleys set to sail around the southern tip of Italy and into Africa. Brindisi was an old Greek city named for its deer-shaped natural harbor. It had been taken by the Romans fifty years ago, but even still, it was clear that the locals didn't think of themselves as Romans.

Massinissa shifted on his horse.

"We should be loaded within the hour," Scipio said. Both of them were eager to leave this town where they were strangers. Their welcome here had been lukewarm at best, and whatever hospitality they had been shown had only been because of the legions of Roman soldiers camped all around the city.

They watched in silence as the soldiers marched up the gangplanks and onto the ships. The ships rocked gently in the harbor, sheltered from the rougher ocean waves and strong winds they would meet in the next couple of hours. The boats were the best in all of Rome and could withstand anything. Scipio knew that much.

"You will be king of Numidia again. I swear it," Scipio said.

"I know," Massinissa said. His shoulders were straight, his chin was high, and he looked every bit the true king of Numidia.

Scipio felt a prick of conscience for using the Numidian king in order to crush Hannibal, but it had to be done. He turned his eyes back to the harbor. "I met him once, you know."

"You are lucky, Roman."

"Historians will compare Alexander the Great and Hannibal the Conqueror, masters of warfare," Scipio said.

Massinissa smiled, and Scipio wondered if he was reliving his time working with such a man as Hannibal.

"I envy you, you know," Scipio said. "You served with a true commander. I have served with imbeciles. I have learned only from my enemy."

Massinissa looked over at Scipio, his face grave. "In war, your enemies are cities, states, and armies. Ideas and dreams. They are not the men themselves. In battle, all warriors are brothers." He kicked his horse to a walk and began the slow trek down the hill to the harbor.

Scipio watched him go. Did he regret joining ranks with the Roman army? Word from Cannae had it that Varro and Paulus had lost so viciously that if they hadn't died in battle, they'd have fallen on their swords. They had never been a good team, even in the Senate. They couldn't agree on a coherent plan and undermined each other at every move. Scipio was determined that he and Massinissa would work much more cohesively together.

CHAPTER 74

Outside the City Walls of Zama, Africa

The sand was bleached white under the sun and palm fronds bent in the breeze, bowing to the 30-foot thick walls and the pillars that rose above them on the other side. Zama was a tropical paradise of the gods, but in this moment, it was all lost amid sixty-thousand Roman soldiers launching fireballs over her walls.

Scipio and Massinissa sat atop their mounts and watched as flames rose from inside the city to lick the perfect sky.

"Is it difficult to watch your city burn?" Scipio asked. The moment the words were out of his mouth, he wished he could take them back. Of course it was hard. The thought of Rome burning made him feel sick.

"At the moment, it's not my city," Massinissa said, his face impassive.

A side gate opened outward from the city, and a detachment of cavalry exited. In the middle of the group was a coach, gilded in gold and pulled by fine black horses.

Scipio turned to the soldiers who waited behind him. "Capture the caravan. Alive if possible. Bring me the survivors."

Massinissa shook his head. "No," he said. "That's not necessary."

"But that must be Scyla and his new bride."

"I know where they're headed." The tired lines around his eyes deepened.

The moment the caravan carrying the pretender had disappeared up the road, the city gate opened once again. A Numidian riot poured through the gate, but they didn't hold weapons. In their hands, they waved olive branches.

Massinissa sat straighter, and his eyes came to life with the joy that his people still recognized him as their king. He looked at Scipio.

"This is your moment," Scipio said, extending his hand to the welcoming mob.

Massinissa spurred his horse and galloped toward his home.

CHAPTER 75

Barca Compound, Carthage

Sophonisba heard a carriage pull up in front of the compound and got up to see who it was. Her heart pounded. What now? News of her husband? She wasn't sure she could handle any more while she still grieved Lady Barca and Hasdrubal.

An unfamiliar guard opened the carriage door and helped Scyla and Sapanibal down. Even in the dark, Sophonisba recognized the fear set into her young sister's shoulders.

As soon as they disappeared from view, a loud pounding issued forth from the front door downstairs.

Sophonisba stepped out on her balcony in time to watch the servants struggling to secure the front door against Scyla's savage pounding.

"I am the King of Numidia, and this is the house of my wife!" Scyla shouted. "Let me in, now!"

Something must have happened in Zama. She wondered if Hannibal was back in Africa. She wondered if she should hope he was, hope that he had defeated the Romans, returned to Africa, and restored Massinissa. But she knew better than that. Word had it that Massinissa had defected to the Romans in order to get his kingdom back. If Scyla was here, then Rome, not Hannibal, was nearly at their doorstep. Scyla would be able to tell her the news.

"Open the door," Sophonisba said to the servants.

The servants unbarred the door, and it slammed back against the wall. The servants both jumped back, eager to be unseen. Scyla rushed in with Sapanibal close behind.

The servants rushed to relatch the door.

Scyla turned and glared at them. "My guards are still outside."

"No foreign soldiers are welcome in the house of Barca," Sophonisba said. Scyla the pretender, after all, was no soldier. She wondered if he would even understand her insult.

Scyla looked all around him before thinking to look up. He met Sophonisba's eyes. She didn't budge. She would put up with the scoundrel until he told her what she needed to hear, but she wouldn't offer him any privileges.

"I need my guards," Scyla said again. "You have your servants open this door right now."

"The next time those doors open will be to send you away."

Scyla scowled and dropped his gaze. "Show us to our room," he said to the nearest servant.

Sophonisba left the balcony and descended the stairs.

As soon as she was on ground level, Sapanibal raced to Sophonisba and buried her face against Sophonisba's shoulder.

"It was horrible," she said. "There were balls of fire flying over the walls. The whole city was burning. We were besieged."

Sophonisba patted Sapanibal's hair and rubbed her back for a moment. The girl cried harder, adding fuel to Sophonisba's rage. Scyla thought he was so conniving, but he hadn't thought through the fact that Massinissa wasn't an easy man to betray. Now with Rome behind him, there was no way little Scyla would keep his throne. What a fool. He cast his lot with Ida Hanna in the Council, but now that reality has struck home, he comes running for the Barca's help.

"There, there," Sophonisba said in Sapanibal's ear. "Why don't you go upstairs? Your bed is ready. Have a bath. I'm preparing a gift for you." She gestured for a servant to take Sapanibal up to her old room.

It was time to have a little talk with Scyla.

"Bring wine," she directed the other servant. Then she looked over at Scyla, who stood at the base of the stairs, about to follow his wife. "You must be tired from your arduous journey. A little wine to unwind?" She worked hard to keep the disdain from her voice.

He turned away from the stairs. "Thank you."

The servant brought wine and Sophonisba motioned for Scyla to follow her into the sitting room.

The servant poured them each glasses.

Scyla seated himself in the tallest chair in the room.

The tallest chair for the smallest man, Sophonisba thought. "I take it the siege did not end well," she said. She wandered over to the mantel, where a fire poker rested. She picked it up and stoked the fire back to life. She wondered how it would feel to put the poker through Scyla's face. It was dull. He would bleed for a long time before he died. The blood might never come out of the sitting room rug, which, though plain, had been in the Barca family for six generations. This was already a big enough mess to clean up. She set the poker down.

"The Romans took the city. No doubt Massinissa is already on my throne," Scyla said.

"Surely Carthage will come to your aid." The sarcasm oozed out despite her best efforts, but Scyla didn't seem to notice her tone.

"Ha!" he said, slamming his goblet of wine down on the table next to the chair. "Ida Hanna has no army. I'm turning to the Barcas, my blood through marriage. I will wait for Hannibal's return, and he will restore my kingdom."

Sophonisba wandered to the other side of the room, where a suit of armor decorated the windowless wall. A knife was stuck into the side of the armor, and she pulled it out and studied the point. The metal gleamed in the light from the lamp and the fireplace across the room. "Hannibal would restore a pretender with no army to his throne?"

"Why else would I have married into the family of the sword and spear?" Scyla said, like this should have been obvious.

"You sound very certain," Sophonisba said. She grasped the hilt of the knife and turned it over in her hand, testing its weight.

"If he ever wants to see his family again, he will do as I say. My guards will be waiting outside the compound for him to return. He shall not enter until he agrees to restore my throne."

"Massinissa was his friend," Sophonisba said. She scraped the knife gently against her finger. It was sharp enough to make a clean kill.

"Not anymore. He defected to Rome. That makes Massinissa his enemy," Scyla said, as though she was a child who knew nothing. "Now Hannibal will be my ally."

"For some, allies are pieces on a game board. Quickly shifted, quickly forgotten," she said. "Others do not play such games."

"I don't think you understand the gravity of your position." He took a giant swig of wine.

"Perhaps there is a lack of understanding," Sophonisba said. She walked toward him pausing behind his chair.

His voice dripped with superiority. "I am a very dangerous man."

"What an honor to have such a dangerous man as a guest of the house of sword and spear." Rage built in her. How dare he threaten her?

He took another large swig of wine.

Sophonisba continued, "Let us teach you our ways." She reached over the back of his chair with her knife hand and jammed the blade hard into his throat.

His goblet fell from his hand, spilled across the side table and clattered loudly as it hit the floor.

Blood gurgled in his throat for a moment, and he slumped over in the chair, blood and wine spilling from his mouth into his lap.

One of the servants entered with a new pitcher of wine. "Is everything alright?" he asked.

Sophonisba set the bloody knife on the side table. "More wine, please. After you help me get this body upstairs."

The servant came further into the room and gasped. "He's—"

"Dead," Sophonisba said. "Yes. Quickly now, before he has a chance to stain the rug."

They carried little Scyla up the stairs and threw him out the window on top of his guards waiting in the street directly below. As they cried out in shock and fear, Sophonisba washed her hands and went to check on her sleeping children.

CHAPTER 76

Campagna Coast, Italy

Hannibal dismounted and led his horse to the edge of the water. Without giving himself a chance to second guess his decision, he drew his sword and slit the horse's neck in one swift strike. The horse slumped and fell forward, stumbling into the sea, lifeless.

Maherabal rode up behind him. The rest of the Carthaginian army marched rapidly toward the sea.

"Kill the horses and the elephants," Hannibal said. "We need to be boarding the ships before nightfall."

"Sir, the ships haven't arrived," Maherabal said.

"They will." Hannibal looked out over the empty horizon, watching his dead horse bob away on the waves in his periphery. He felt a pang. It had been a good horse and hadn't deserved to die, but there would be no room on the ships for it or any of the other animals. Rather than leave them behind, they had to kill the animals or the Romans would use them against Carthage.

Maherabal dismounted.

Hannibal walked over to Maherabal's horse and slashed its neck. The horse fell to the ground.

Maherabal flinched. "Where will we find horses for battle?"

"In Africa." He hoped he was right. It was a gamble he had to take.

"But these horses, these elephants, are battle tested. They are invaluable."

The rest of the Sacred Band rode up and pulled to a stop next to the water's edge. They dismounted, and Hannibal went down the line with his sword, slicing each horse's throat quickly. Each horse dropped to its knees, squealing as it bled out.

Maherabal followed him down the line, the left corner of his lip curling down in pain to see each great beast toppled.

"We can defend Carthage with what we have space to bring with us now or we can wait for enough transport to carry our animals and have nothing left to defend," Hannibal said.

Maherabal drew his sword and sliced the last horse's throat. "It will be done," he said.

Hannibal cringed as the last horse fell on the beach and stained the sand with its blood. He didn't like to do this, but like Massinissa, these beasts had been groomed for greatness and would otherwise be his demise. He met Maherabal's eyes and knew that they were both thinking the same thing.

The war elephants arrived on the beach. Their Mahouts slipped down from their backs and grabbed their scythed spears. With tears in their eyes, they sliced the elephants' necks and backed away as they collapsed ingloriously in the sand.

Hannibal stared into the eyes of the closest elephant. It

was courageous even in death. It blinked slowly once, silently accepting its fate. The eyes drooped shut, and the leathery face relaxed into the bloody sand. He wondered if the animals were relieved not to see another battle, and he knelt to send up a prayer that wherever the souls of the beasts resided in the afterlife, it was a finer place than here. *May they have perfect skies and sweet hay and no men with spears and swords*, Hannibal thought.

He rose to his feet and turned his back to the dead beasts lining the shore. His Italian campaign was dead. He could only look toward home now and hope it wasn't too late.

CHAPTER 77

In the Mediterranean Sea

The ship rocked in the rough Mediterranean waves. Torrents of water whipped against the side of the flagship, casting spray over the railing and into Hannibal's face. The entire sky for as far as he could see was a black dome pricked with holes through which tiny flecks of light glowed.

Behind him, hundreds of ships kept pace, each housing his battle-weary troops.

The journey home wasn't the glorious journey they had all hoped for. They had marched over the Iberian plains with jaunty steps and a glow of excitement in their eyes, but gone now was the innocent courage of untested soldiers. They returned home old and tired and with the kind of dogged courage that came from knowing they were closer to death than home for much too long.

There might not be a difference between death and home, Hannibal thought. He turned his eyes to the sky. "Has your favor abandoned Carthage?" he said.

There were no words from the lips of the gods tonight.

Hannibal kept still. Maybe if he looked harder, waited longer.

An asteroid streaked across the sky. It burst into a small explosion of white light and disappeared.

Hannibal closed his eyes. Carthage was that white light, exploding with brilliance and disappearing under the weight of her own greatness. If only Ida Hanna hadn't lusted after her power. If only Hannibal could have kept her people loyal. If only there was any hope left of victory. But this was a useless game.

"Help me," he whispered, hoping there was a god out there who still cared.

CHAPTER 78

African Coast

The moment the flagship ran aground, Hannibal leaped from the deck into the thigh deep water and waded to shore. Standing on land felt strange, dizzying after so many days at sea, and he stumbled over his first few steps before getting his bearings.

Up and down the beach, boats pressed into the sand and stopped.

The Sacred Band was already setting up camp at the highest point of the beach. Maherabal broke away from them and walked down the beach to Hannibal.

"Carthaginian troops, horses, and one hundred war elephants will meet us at camp tonight," Maherabal said. "Should we march to Carthage?"

"No," Hannibal said. "There's no time. Besides, our elephants will be useless hidden behind the city walls. We must choose an open battleground."

"Yes, sir."

"How many reinforcements?"

"Twenty thousand fresh troops," Maherabal said. "That brings our number to thirty-five thousand."

It wasn't enough. Hannibal looked away from Maherabal, watching his men, tired from the journey, drag themselves up the beach to set up camp above the tide line. He strode away to pitch his tent and stew up a battle plan. His boots leaked and slurped with every step. He had to make something work. Carthage depended on it.

CHAPTER 79

Zama

Scipio stood on the lookout tower outside the royal quarters, scanning the horizon. Finally, he saw movement. He blinked, and it was still there, a little bigger this time. It wasn't a mirage. Hannibal's army was rapidly approaching from over the eastern ridgeline. Exhilaration flooded him. This was the moment he'd been waiting for: the chance to fight his most brilliant enemy.

"Form ranks!" Scipio called down from the wall. "Hannibal at the gate!"

The door to the royal quarters opened and Massinissa stepped out into the blaze of the mid-morning sun. "Hannibal's here," he said. He looked up at Scipio with a strange look on his face that hit Scipio like a cold wind and threatened to dampen his excitement. Massinissa and Hannibal were fellow Africans. They had planned to fight this part of the war on the same side.

"Yes," Scipio said. "See to your men."

Massinissa turned away from Scipio and walked stiffly from the wall, calling for his own army to form ranks.

Scipio looked out from the wall once again and saw Hannibal's sure form galloping ahead of his army. A thrill went through him. No matter what happened today, he would remember it until the very end.

CHAPTER 80

Zama

Hannibal halted his troops in the field near Zama within view
of the city gates. His soldiers stood in a phalanx twenty men
deep in order to counter the superior Roman cavalry thrust.
On either wing, he had positioned a cavalry contingent, and
in the back, fifty elephants shifted impatiently under their
Mahouts. He'd thought through every possible strategy, and
had come up between a rock and a hard place. His men needed to rest, but with Rome so close to Carthage, there was no
time. It would take a stroke of luck straight from the hand of
Baal to win this battle.

He glanced over his shoulder and saw Massinissa's troops
advancing from the city. Massinissa gave an order to split his
cavalry force to match Hannibal's on both sides, and the men
obeyed. Scipio's men followed, stacked in an aligned checkerboard according to the typical Roman fashion.

Maherabal waited at Hannibal's left for instructions.

"We'll need fate on our side today," Hannibal said.

"That's how it always is in war," Maherabal said.

"No. This is the first time." In every other battle, Hannibal
had been confident that they could win. This time, he didn't

249

see how Carthage could possibly come out the victor. Rome was superior in numbers and strength, and unlike the previous Roman generals, Scipio was not an idiot.

"Is it Massinissa who worries you?" Maherabal asked.

"I can neutralize Massinissa." He looked over the heads of his men to where the elephants swung their trunks. "I don't know if I can depend on these beasts."

"They're the largest and finest in Africa," Maherabal said.

"I'm sure that's true, but they have never heard the trumpet of a charge or felt the prick of a Roman sword." He faced Maherabal. "Our entire plan depends on them behaving as soldiers."

Maherabal looked up to the sky. "Baal favors Carthage."

Hannibal frowned and watched the puffy clouds pressed across the sky by the sharp wind. The strong gusts suggested a heavy stroke of the gods on the battlefield, but he had no faith that it would stay his way. "Winds are fickle," he said. "The stars do not change."

A soldier jogged up to Hannibal and handed him a spear shaft with a white flag tied to the end of it.

"What are you doing?" Maherabal asked, though everyone knew what the white flag meant.

"I'll sue Scipio for peace." He kept his voice steady and his jaw set. He hadn't reached the decision lightly, and he would not be swayed from it.

"And forsake your struggle, your hatred of Rome?"

"Today, certain peace for Carthage is better than an improbable victory."

"There's truly no hope otherwise?" Maherabal said. "Hope is so grim?"

Hannibal pressed his lips together. He didn't need to respond; Maherabal already knew the answer to that.

"He won't accept it," Maherabal said.

"I have to ask. For Carthage. It is this or rot behind our walls. I won't die hiding." Hannibal spurred his horse. Holding the white flag high, he galloped to the center of the battlefield alone.

CHAPTER 81

Zama

Scipio watched Hannibal ride to the center of the battlefield, peace flag held aloft. Shock flooded him, but he worked to hide it as he mounted his horse, took up a white flag of his own, and trotted to meet Hannibal in the middle of the field.

They each dismounted, dropped their flags by their horses, and approached each other on foot.

"We meet again," Hannibal said.

"Do you regret letting me go now?" Scipio studied Hannibal's face. If anything he looked harder now, fiercer.

"No. For once, I respect the man I'm fighting."

Scipio looked away for a moment. "I am only smart enough to mimic your own tactics. I'm an imitator."

"To good effect," Hannibal said. "Young men imitate. Masters create. What have you created for me today?"

Scipio felt a smile threatening to push through his façade of the calm, collected general. "So you galloped out here under a truce flag in order to ask me about my battle plans?"

Something shifted in the air. "No," Hannibal said. "I came to beg you for peace on behalf of Carthage."

The moment stretched long between them while Scipio

tried to wrap his mind around the fact that the great General Hannibal Barca was begging him to forsake battle. What kind of strategy was he playing at now? It must be a trap, for the great Hannibal Barca never backed down from a battle. No battle was too hopeless for him to win.

"Of all the commanders that Rome has sent against you, I am the first to hear those words," Scipio said, guarding his words carefully.

"Carthage is weary from war. Her people are divided and her coffers are bare. Let us go home. Let us remember and renew the terms of the treaty from the first war."

Scipio scrutinized Hannibal's face. The older man didn't so much as twitch. Only a slight pucker of his eyebrows gave away his own shame at asking for such a thing. "Carthage begs for peace, but what does Hannibal beg for?"

Hannibal said nothing.

"Hannibal doesn't beg, does he?" Scipio said.

"I come to you as an emissary of Carthage."

Scipio stilled for a second, and a sudden burst of anger filled him. Hannibal Barca could not back down in such a manner. It wasn't right. And what would the old senators say if he came all this way only to return to Rome with a peace treaty? They wouldn't like it. They'd call him foolish. Here he was so close to winning. Hannibal wouldn't ask for peace if he believed he could still win.

Scipio swung up on his horse. "You know as well as I do the ancient codes of warfare. One does not negotiate until the fighting is finished. It would be dishonorable to both of us." The words came out like sharp blades.

Hannibal kept his chin high and didn't break eye contact.

"My former ally is not your friend."

Did he mean Massinissa? Was this a scare tactic or a fair warning? Scipio glowered. No. He wouldn't back down. He wanted his battle. After so many hopeless battles with the incompetent Roman generals who had practically handed Hannibal victories, Scipio wanted to have his chance.

"Rome doesn't need friends," Scipio said. "Your former allies are more than enough."

He kicked his horse and galloped away without looking back.

CHAPTER 82

Zama

Hannibal watched Scipio go. He wasn't surprised at his response. Dread filled him, but it was mixed with relief. Hannibal was willing to do anything he could to preserve Carthage, but giving up a chance to slay Romans sickened him.

No, it was better this way.

He mounted his horse and gazed into the distance where the Roman lines waited.

He shook his head. Somehow, this day would pass, but there was no telling where it would find him. He couldn't think about that right now.

He trotted back to his own lines and dismounted. He faced his center line and stepped forward to clasp hands with several of them. He walked between his men as he spoke, feeling their weariness permeate the air around him.

"Men of Carthage, we have reached the end of our arduous journey. We have defeated every Roman force put in front of our blades. And now we stand with all that we love at our backs. Here we battle for the survival of our home and country. If Carthage is destroyed, then all that will remain is hatred."

As he spoke, he felt the energy level around him rising. They were weary from travel and battle, but their spirits were not yet broken. There was still some hope left.

"Every man is measured," Hannibal continued, "by purpose in life and honor in death."

"The Roman cavalry is advancing!" Maherabal shouted from the front of the center line.

"Lions of Carthage!" Hannibal shouted. He turned and strode toward Maherabal.

The veterans around him rumbled with guttural approval. It was time to fight for what was theirs. Hannibal felt strength pouring through him at the sound of their support. He swung up on his horse once again and looked to Maherabal for further details.

"Our cavalry already have their orders," Maherabal said.

"Send them," Hannibal said. This was it. He felt his mind emptying of everything but the battle in front of him. This battle was the only thing that existed in the world.

Maherabal galloped off, flagging to each of the cavalry captains on the Carthaginian flanks.

"Let's test Massinissa's pride," Hannibal said, to no one in particular.

The Carthaginian cavalry cantered to meet Massinissa's much larger force.

The moment Hannibal saw Massinissa's fierce expression he realized that not only was his former friend's pride still intact, but he intended with every breath in his body to win. It was enough to almost scare him. But Hannibal intended to win as well. He raced along with his cavalry, hearing the concussion the moment his men hit spears with the Numidians.

Hannibal held back, waiting for Scipio's call to charge and watching the skirmish with a calculating eye. Within minutes, the Carthaginians began to fall back. They were not strong enough in numbers or morale to beat back Massinissa's fresh troops who had recently reclaimed their homeland with very little injury to their own numbers.

As the Carthaginian cavalry turned tail and fled, the Numidians pursued them to the other side of the battlefield and into the brush.

"Cut them down! Let none escape!" Massinissa's shout was barely discernible over the thousands of hoof beats and clashing of spears.

Hannibal's mind worked in rapid calculations. With Massinissa's troops pursuing his cavalry, it left only Scipio's forces to bring down. Everything was progressing according to plan, it could work. There was no time to worry.

As the Numidian cavalry disappeared from sight, Hannibal gave the signal to his infantry captain. He felt his smirk showing, and the captain of the infantry stood up straighter at the sight of it.

Good, Hannibal thought. Confidence could only help them.

"Double forward march!" the infantry captain called.

The entire Carthaginian line stood straighter and stepped forward in unison. They marched forward in a block formation perfectly in tune with each other. Their eyes glinted brighter than their weapons, and the ferocity of lions shone in their faces. The sight of them was enough to send chills down even the most seasoned veteran's back, and to make an unseasoned warrior shit himself.

"Lions of Carthage!" Hannibal called out as he rode alongside them and circled around them to lead the attack.

CHAPTER 83

Zama

Scipio saw the Carthaginian infantry rapidly approaching, their steps synchronized in their motions as well as their determination. Their armor reflected the hard sunlight, and the purple standard of Carthage waved in the air like a dare. Hannibal Barca rode ahead of them all, yelling as he led the charge, his every movement calculated and strong like a feral animal.

Worry sprouted in Scipio's chest. Massinissa and his troops were already across the field, pursuing the fleeing Carthaginian cavalry. Without Massinissa, Scipio's strategy had only nominal chance of success. He beckoned a member of his guard.

"Send riders out to bring Massinissa back," he said. And then to his captain, he said, "We stand no chance without him. Hold our infantry back. Delay conflict until he returns."

The guard raced off, and moments later, a group of riders sped across the battlefield.

But Hannibal had doubled his advance. No matter how quickly Massinissa returned to the field, it wouldn't be fast enough.

"Hold them!" Scipio shouted.

"Charge!" yelled the captain of Hannibal's infantry.

Roman shields went up, and the Carthaginians ran into them with the ringing of hundreds of spears and swords smashing through Roman armor.

Scipio stood with his front lines, swiftly felling several men. He turned to take out a fifth and saw that already his men were falling back. The Carthaginians fought more ferociously here on their own African soil than they had fought in Rome. Had Hannibal been messing with his head by first begging for a truce? The great Hannibal Barca must have known that Scipio would refuse him. Had he been played? Surely not! After all, everything Hannibal had said about his tired, diminished numbers was true.

But it was time for action, not rumination.

"Hold them steady!" Scipio shouted. "No retreat! Your honor, men! You are warriors!"

CHAPTER 84

Zama

"Push! Break their formations!" Hannibal shouted. They pushed the Romans back on their heels step by step, crunching the front maniples into those behind them and shoving their checkerboard pattern together tightly enough to make mobility more difficult.

It was working so far, and now was the time to bring out the elephants. If it had been their tested and true elephants from the Italian campaign, Hannibal wouldn't have hesitated, but these fresh beasts…anything could happen.

"Now is the time, sir," Maherabal said from behind his right ear. "Before Massinissa returns."

He was right. It was now or never. His infantry wouldn't be able to keep pushing the Romans back long enough to gain victory.

"Call them in," Hannibal said. "May Baal guide our fortune."

"Elephants!" Maherabal called.

On his order, fifty war elephants rode up from behind, already bleating in panic from the unnatural noises of war around them.

Hannibal rode out to the side in order to get a better view of the battle. He watched the elephants rampage toward the back of the Carthaginian line, and his stomach clenched. These elephants weren't ready for this. But they would have to make it work. "Make holes!" he shouted.

The lines of the infantry block shifted to make holes in the lines for the elephants to barrel through.

Across the field, Hannibal heard Scipio's call. "Legions form columns! Prepare for the elephants!"

The Roman checkerboard shifted, forming vertical columns that allowed the elephants to pass between them with minimal injury. The Romans pulled out long spears the length of nearly four men stacked on top of each other. Razor sharp scythes and hooked ends graced the tops of the spears.

Hannibal's stomach clenched harder. Of course Scipio's men were prepared for elephants. He had seen the devastating losses in the Italian countryside. The elephants crashed through the Carthaginian holes and aimed themselves at the empty space between the Romans' vertical columns. Their Mahouts struggled to maintain control.

The Romans took turns dashing out with their scythes aimed at the elephants' soft bellies. An elephant, startled by the pain, screamed and stomped. Other Romans used the hooks to drag the Mahouts from atop the elephants. Shrieks lit the air. Hannibal couldn't tell if it was man or beast.

One Roman dragged a Mahout from his perch and the Mahout fell face first in the dirt. His terrified elephant flailed to the left and crushed the man's skull under its enormous feet.

Another elephant swung its trunk viciously into a Roman

soldier only to have another Roman race forward and slice the trunk almost clean off the beast's face. The beast belted out a horrible sucking sound and plowed into one of the Roman columns, blindly pushing through men as they pricked it on its way by. It became so disoriented by the pricking and slashing and pain that it circled back and rampaged back into the Carthaginian line.

"Pull the elephants back!" Hannibal shouted. "Keep them under control!"

But it was too late. Only half of the Mahouts were still sitting atop their perches, and even fewer of them had any control over their elephants and clung to the wooden beams that served as a basket to hold a man and his weapons.

More and more elephants started circling around in their frenzy, charging indiscriminately at whatever space seemed to have the least number of men.

"Pull back!" Hannibal shouted.

No sooner were the words out of his mouth than the lead elephant reared up on his hind legs. The Mahout was flung backward and slammed into the ground so hard that he didn't move again. The elephant's scream filled the air. Its front legs paddled in front of it, as though it might kick off into the sky.

When its front feet touched the ground again, it flung itself in the opposite direction and plunged back toward the Carthaginian line, bringing with it the rest of the herd.

"Make holes!" Hannibal shouted. "Let them through the line!" But his words weren't able to create enough space. The elephants charged the line through the heart of the phalanx, stomping down any man who didn't move away fast enough.

But everywhere the elephants turned there were men

with weapons. Some of the animals again spun around and charged the Roman lines, bouncing between the soldiers. Terror was their guide, with Carthage now taking the brunt of their own animals.

The one solace Hannibal could take in that moment, and it was only the faintest flicker of one, was that for however long the elephant rampage lasted, Carthage and Rome were united against a common foe. They had stopped fighting each other and instead focused their energy on dodging the elephants' feet and trunks and creating openings for them to escape from the field.

When at last the elephants had retreated beyond the battlefield, Maherabal gave the cry: "Forward charge!"

The cry for order sent a ripple of energy through the shocked and exhausted Carthaginians. They straightened and rushed at the Romans with renewed vigor, pushing them back several paces. Carthage could yet win this battle, and this hope savaged the Roman line.

CHAPTER 85

Zama

Scipio barked orders with renewed fury, but his troops were falling back no matter what he shouted. Bitterness filled him as he realized that Hannibal was snatching victory from his clutches. He had been so confident, but even though the elephants had backfired, Carthage was still managing to pull ahead. Scipio's grudging admiration warred with his pride.

He squinted out over the horizon and saw a cloud of dust growing on the horizon.

"Massinissa!" he yelled. The warrior king and his cavalry returned from the opposite side of the field, hemming the Carthaginians in on the front and back.

His men, nearly falling over on each other, perked up at this. If Massinissa was back, then the tides of war were moving back in Rome's favor.

CHAPTER 86

Zama

The moment Hannibal saw the cloud of dust approaching from behind the Carthaginian lines, he realized that they were finished. He felt the blood drain from his face, and the calculating calm that usually stole over him during battle was replaced by a maniacal urgency to inflict as much destruction as he could before Massinissa's cavalry came and finished them off.

Hannibal threw himself into the heart of the battle, pulling out his sword and hacking apart two Romans in a single stroke. When someone tried to grab him off his horse, he reached behind him, grabbed the man's neck, threw the man forward into his waiting sword, and then punted him off of his blade. The now-dead Roman slammed into his fellow soldiers with enough force to send four men staggering to the ground under him.

When the cavalry was nearly visible through the spaces in his line, he spun, whipping the head off of a Roman officer, and turned to the nearest member of the Sacred Band. "Remove my family from the city," he ordered.

Maherabal pointed at three Sacred Band members, and

they spun their horses and galloped away to Carthage, narrowly missing being slammed by Massinissa's cavalry.

The Numidian cavalry fought its way through Hannibal's line, leaving carnage in its wake.

This was it, Hannibal knew. There was nothing more they could do here. His men were falling like nothing more than heads of grain in a field meeting the scythe. There was nothing that could win this battle for them.

"Retreat!" Hannibal called out. "Fall back to Carthage! Make our last stand on the city walls."

He spurred his horse and galloped toward Carthage with the Sacred Band trailing him, and his men desperately beating through Massinissa's cavalry in an attempt to follow him.

CHAPTER 87

Barca Compound

Sophonisba watched the three soldiers galloping up the street in full armor. She looked for any sign that one of them was her husband, but she didn't recognize his frame among them. Her heart stammered when she saw the crests of their helmets; they were members from Hannibal's Sacred Guard. She raced downstairs and opened the door to the compound. They pulled up in front of her, and she motioned them in quickly, shutting and barring the door after them.

"Come in and have a drink," she said.

"There's no time," said the shortest of the three men. His shoulders were straight and tense, but his eyes made him look far older than he was. All of Hannibal's guard had left Carthage while in their prime, and all of them were returning as very old men.

"What's happened?" she asked, fear nipping at her stomach. "Hannibal isn't…?" she couldn't bring herself to say the word. *Dead.*

"No. We are here on his orders to get you out of the city before the Romans arrive," the man said.

Relief flooded her, and trepidation followed closely on its

heels. She already knew the Romans were in Africa, but now Hannibal had returned. "Where is my husband?" The battle couldn't possibly be going well if the orders were to flee the city. Would she see him again?

A rapping sound came at the door, and the guards opened it and admitted an armored carriage to the compound.

"Scipio and Massinissa are chasing our men all the way to Carthage. The plan is to make the last stand on the city walls, but…" the shorter man trailed off.

He didn't need to finish. Sophonisba had filled in all the details herself. It didn't look good for Carthage or Hannibal.

"Massinissa is coming?" said a voice from the front door of the house. Sapanibal approached, timid and wringing the fabric of her robe in either hand. Her brow was raised, tinged with hope.

"He's the one destroying Carthage and about to kill your brother," Sophonisba snapped. "Gather the children. We must leave instantly."

Sapanibal inhaled as though to say something but then lost heart. She turned and went back into the house, calling for Hamilcar and Didobal to come quickly.

Sophonisba raced inside the house and grabbed a handful of important things: food for the children, blankets, and General Hamilcar's collection of maps. She called to the servants, and the members of the household climbed aboard the carriage.

Didobal cried out as the carriage jerked forward. Sophonisba grabbed her from Sapanibal and held her close, stroking her soft baby cheek and whispering that everything was going to be okay.

CHAPTER 88

Carthage, Front Gate

Hannibal rode with all his might to Carthage, surrounded by the remaining members of the Sacred Band and the soldiers with enough energy or adrenaline pumping in their veins to stay close at his heels. As he rounded the crest of the hill that sloped down to the harbor, he saw Massinissa's cavalry neck and neck with them. It would be a close race.

His only thought was to make it to the front gate before Massinissa. He had to close it before the Numidian cavalry flooded the city and sealed the city's fall. Everything hinged on getting to that door.

His heart beat in time with his thoughts. *The door. The door. The door.*

It got closer.

Closer.

He reached out.

His fingers touched the wood and still he rode forward, pushing the gate closed.

It was heavy and slow.

Massinissa gave a shout from behind Hannibal's ear. Though it didn't break his concentration, it didn't matter. He was already through the gate, followed by a stream of Numidian cavalry, who slashed their spears at Hannibal.

He was forced to let go of the door or have his arms cut off. He ducked under one spear, dodged the next, and spurred his horse forward into the city walls. He was surrounded by his men, who struggled to beat off the Numidians before they became too many.

CHAPTER 89

Carthaginian Council Chamber

Hannibal dismounted on the steps of the council chamber. Maherabal jumped down from his horse next to him, and the other members of the Sacred Band dismounted and surrounded them, slaying all Numidians audacious enough to storm the capitol building.

Hannibal entered the building with Maherabal at his right hand.

Ida Hanna exited the council chamber. Ida stopped walking when he saw Hannibal. His expression was equal parts self-satisfied and fearful, as if he was pleased to witness Hannibal's failure while knowing the defeat was shared by them both.

"If you are here, then all is lost," Ida said. "Carthage was wrong to trust the house of Barca!"

Ida was not wrong. Anger flushed itself from Hannibal's heart and into his hands. He whipped out two swords and crossed them in front of his face, weighing his options.

Ida's eyes flashed with surprise.

But why should he be surprised, Hannibal thought bitterly. If it hadn't been for Ida's treachery, Carthage would have won the war against Rome. With this final thought, he back-handed the left sword blade through Ida's neck and stuck him through the face to the wall behind him.

Ida's head hung trapped against the wall, afraid for a moment even to bleed. His body slumped to the ground, spurting blood like a hot spring.

"At least Carthage will outlive you."

CHAPTER 90

Front Gate

The carriage thundered down the streets to the front gate, but Sophonisba knew that it was already too late. Battle cries vibrated through the air, and she could hear the clink of weapons. She dared a peek out the window to catch one last glimpse of her husband. What if she never saw him again? It seemed unlikely that she would. Even if the carriage, by some stroke of luck, made it out of the city, Hannibal surely wouldn't.

She buried her face in Didobal's curls and clutched Hamilcar's chubby hand.

The carriage suddenly halted.

"No one leaves the city!" a familiar voice said.

Sapanibal sat up in her seat and pulled the covering back from the window. "Massinissa?" she exclaimed, standing partway.

Sophonisba jerked her back down, but Massinissa had seen them. He slashed down a few members of the Sacred Band and the young Carthaginian guards who tried to stand in his way. They were inexperienced and no match against the battle-hardened general and his men.

The carriage door opened, and the Numidian king looked inside at what was left of the mighty Barca family, all cramped into the tiny space. He paused.

Sophonisba held her breath. He could kill them. This was war, and that's what happened during war. But she saw his eyes soften when they landed on Sapanibal. He looked at her for too long, and she gazed back at him, imploringly. Tears beaded up in her eyes but didn't fall.

"Stay here," he said. He closed the door behind him. "Drive this carriage. Follow me," he said to an unseen man.

Again, the carriage jerked forward. Sophonisba risked a tiny peek from a crack in the curtain. She saw the carriage pass through the city walls and through what seemed like the entire Numidian cavalry, until the clanking of weapons had receded, and there was only a scrubby path and an astonishingly turquoise view of the sea.

CHAPTER 91

Council Chamber Building Steps

From the steps, Hannibal watched a fresh onslaught of Numidian cavalry make the final turn toward the capitol building. Two dozen of the Sacred Band stood around him, exchanging looks and steeling their poise for what they all knew would be their last stand as brothers and as countrymen.

The Numidians broke into a charge.

Hannibal crouched, readying himself for impact. Was he ready to die? Was this what it felt like to stare certain death in the face? The scent of orange blossoms floated on the breeze. Armor clanked. Men shouted. Overhead a gull cried. His pulse hammered in his neck. Every sense felt sharper than it had ever been.

How was it that he felt so alive when death stood loomed so near? It was as if the gods were telling him that he was not to enter into eternity until he first fought with everything he had left. His grip tightened around his sword.

Maherabal stepped up beside him. "You will not die before me."

The Numidians crashed into the Sacred Band, ten of them to every one Carthaginian.

Hannibal felt the lion of Carthage in his soul beating its way out with every vicious blow he struck against a Numidian neck. With each thrust, he snarled like a rabid animal.

Around him, his brothers fell. One of the Sacred Band fell against Hannibal, throwing him off balance. Hannibal looked down and, for the briefest of moments, their eyes met. Though no sound came out, the man's lips moved forming the words, "Lion of Carthage." The man was dead before his face hit the ground.

Hannibal stepped on the body and used his comrade as leverage to throw himself at three Numidians at once. He plowed them all down with one blow of his sword.

But they kept coming.

For every three he took out, another four appeared to replace them.

The Sacred Band fought harder than Hannibal had ever seen, wildly hacking heads off of shoulders, several at a time, and leaping stairs and fallen bodies to impale enemy hearts on swords. One member of the Sacred Band kicked his horse hard until it reared, screaming, smashing several enemies in the head with its hooves.

Hannibal's muscles burned, reminding him that he was still alive. The sun sank low and orange over the rooftops. Somehow, they'd held off the Numidians for most of the afternoon, but the Sacred Band's numbers dwindled, and the enemy's did not.

Soon, Hannibal and Maherabal were the only ones left. Their only hope was to kill as many Numidians as they could before they followed the sun. A final epitaph. Bones crunched with each step Hannibal took. He refused to look down, preferring to believe that it was Numidian bones he stomped upon. Turncoat Numidians. But it was Ida Hanna's fault. Hannibal's rage would never dampen. He wished he could kill Ida Hanna a hundred times. Ida Hanna and the Romans. Instead, he was left with the Numidians. His old ally. The world is cruel, he thought.

Hannibal turned again, ripping into flesh with his sword. His weapon emerged from the falling corpse, dripping with such volume that it appeared to be bleeding itself.

Maherabal fought tirelessly in front of him.

Just then, a spear flew through the air and soared through Maherabal's left shoulder. Maherabal's sword dropped as his left hand lost the ability to move. Still, he fought, placing desperate, right-handed blows at every figure that approached his periphery. But he could no longer block from his left side and took a blade to the chest once, and then twice.

Hannibal felt his stomach drop from his body as he watched Maherabal struggle to stand and tumble into the pile of bodies under his feet.

"Noooo!" The voice bit through the clash and shrieks of the battle, an unrecognizable snarl. A wild call. This was it. Hannibal whipped his sword around, the edges, now dull from the chink of armor and bone, ripping through flesh in painful, ragged strips.

All he had was one more swing of the sword.

And one more.

And one more.

And one more.

CHAPTER 92

Council Chamber Building Steps

Scipio arrived at the steps of the Carthaginian chamber building in time to see General Hannibal standing alone against fifty Numidians, bravely fighting to his last breath. Awe washed over him. If only they had fought under the same flag. A man like Hannibal didn't deserve to die for a city that betrayed him. It wasn't right. Anger surged over Scipio.

"Spare the General!" he shouted to the Numidians. His voice carried, but they didn't hear. He kicked his horse forward until he stood at the bottom of the steps up to the Chamber. "By order of Rome, leave Hannibal alive!"

The Numidians didn't stop pushing Hannibal back against the wall of the building. Hannibal fended off the blows with a sword in each hand, but it was him against an entire company.

Hannibal took a blow to the neck with a sharp blade, ducking barely enough to not lose his head. Rivulets of blood streamed down his face, and when he swung his sword, Scipio caught a glimpse of the blood that drenched his hands.

Scipio looked behind him and nodded to his captain.

The Latin Cavalry charged the Numidians, pushing into

their backs and creating a path for Scipio.

Scipio rode up the steps. He tugged Hannibal's bloody body from the Numidians' grasp and slung him up on his horse in front of him. Then he galloped away from the Chamber.

"I must die with Carthage," Hannibal said. The words came out forcefully for one who bled so profusely. His eyes rolled back in his head. He blinked and refocused on Scipio's face.

Blood streamed from Hannibal's crown and leaked from his mouth. Was he too weak to wipe it away? His body was a dead weight over Scipio's lap, and his head bounced in rhythm with the horse's gait.

"Carthage has already died without you," Scipio said. "An ungrateful city does not deserve your bones."

Scipio saw a ferocious objection rise on Hannibal's lips, but his eyes glazed, and he was unable to fight anymore. He slumped down, and his head lolled against the side of the horse. Scipio held him firmly in place as he charged through the city gates.

CHAPTER 93

African Coast

Hamilcar plucked his head from Sophonisba's side the moment the carriage stopped. His eyes popped open, and he looked up at her.

"Mommy, are we going home?" he asked.

Sophonisba's heart shattered for the hundredth time today as she looked into the little boy's innocent eyes. "No, sweet one."

"Where are we going?"

The carriage door was opened from the outside, saving Sophonisba from attempting an answer. Massinissa stood on the other side of the door with his hand outstretched.

Sophonisba hesitated.

"Quickly. There's no time to lose. No one must know where you've gone," Massinissa said.

"Is Hannibal dead?" she blurted out.

Massinissa's face remained impassive.

Perhaps he didn't know. Still, if he had meant to kill her, he'd have done it already. She took his hand. He helped her down from the carriage and swung Hamilcar down beside her.

She faced the African shore. The view was much like that from her bedroom window in Carthage, but the light was blinding here, and no city surrounded her. Scrubby bushes and yucca trees stretched as far as she could see, and in the distance, a stand of acacia trees appeared to bow over the water. Reminders of Carthage. The beginning of a lifetime of remembrance, she thought.

They had stopped near a small harbor where a trireme waited, bobbing on the water. Three rows of oars hung still in the water from holes in the side of the boat. Along the dock, sailors moved quickly, carrying supplies onboard. They weren't military. Was Massinissa sending them away? But she couldn't leave without knowing what had befallen Hannibal.

She turned back to Massinissa.

He took Sapanibal's hand and helped her from the carriage. The tears that she'd held back for the duration of the trip still refused to fall. He didn't let go of her hand immediately.

"I didn't want this," Sapanibal said, the words coming out strained but clear.

They gazed into each other's eyes for a long moment.

Finally, Massinissa spoke. "I didn't either." The words sounded choked.

Sophonisba watched in awe while the Numidian king struggled against his own emotions and her sister stood strongly before him. How very changed Sapanibal was.

Massinissa bit his lips and blinked hard, seeming to bring his emotions under control. "In times of war, many decisions are made for us. We can only make the best of what remains."

"Tell me. What does one do when nothing remains?" Sapanibal asked.

Massinissa turned Sapanibal's hand over and brought her palm gently to his chest. "The King of Numidia once asked you to be his queen. Nothing has changed."

Hope bloomed on her face. The tears she'd been holding back dropped down her smooth cheeks. "You would still have me?"

"It would be my honor," he said. He drew her to his chest and lowered his head to kiss her tenderly.

Weeping, she leaned against him, letting his lips graze her forehead and then raising her face to his. He cradled her neck in his right hand and his mouth met hers gently.

Sophonisba looked away. The pain in her heart was almost too much to handle. How she longed for her husband's embrace! How she despised not knowing if he lived or if she would ever feel his lips against hers or his strong hands caress her neck. She closed her eyes and swallowed hard, feeling a lump in her throat that might tear her heart to pieces.

Didobal's little hands patted Sophonisba's face, and she opened her eyes. "Mama," the little girl cooed. She burbled, and spit leaked down her chin.

Sophonisba kissed her cheek.

A movement in her periphery caught her eye. She turned and saw a rider in the distance carrying a lopsided burden. The rider wore Roman red. He came closer and pulled the horse to a stop next to the carriage.

All at once, Sophonisba saw Hannibal, bloodied and barely conscious, but still alive. Her heart thundered, and though all she wanted to do was run to him, she felt rooted to the spot.

Scipio helped him from his horse. "These men will take you to Greece, where you have friends."

"There is no honor in this," Hannibal snapped, but he didn't struggle.

How badly had he been hurt? Sophonisba wondered.

"There is honor in a long, peaceful life," Scipio said.

"I wouldn't allow you the same," Hannibal said.

"You did," Massinissa said.

Hannibal turned slowly, taking in the Numidian King with his arm around Sapanibal. His fiery gaze jumped back to Sophonisba, and their eyes met for the first time since Saguntum. The fire at Scipio's words left him then, and Sophonisba saw only relief in his expression. He stumbled a few steps forward and she came the rest of the way, taking him in her free arm.

He slumped against her, and she felt the wetness of his blood against her neck, mixed with his tears. She'd never let go again.

CHAPTER 94

African Coast

Scipio stood at the edge of the dock and watched the trireme disembark. Strong wind filled out the sails, and the sun flew at half mast, rendering the boat and its passengers red and golden. General Hannibal stood at the railing watching the African shore grow smaller. His wife handed him the child in her arms, and the great general rested his cheek against the baby's hair. He watched the receding shores of his homeland, frozen like a statue.

CHAPTER 95

Carthage

Scipio razed the once magnificent city of Carthage, setting it aflame and scattering every stone from the walls into the countryside. His legionnaires stripped every man-made edifice to the ground, leaving nothing but a layer of rubble.

As the Romans raked through Carthage's ashes, they poured salt into the soil, reducing what once had been the city of the gods, the pearl of Africa, to an uninhabitable wasteland.

There would be no rebirth for Carthage.

EPILOGUE

The old man crouched over the desk, still writing. The candle had burned to a nub, seconds from drowning in wax.

Footsteps thumped, and swords clanked against armor outside the room. The man wrote faster, determination etched into the lines along his forehead and lips. The thunder of soldiers' feet grew louder and stopped outside the door.

A voice boomed from the other side. "Hannibal Barca, you are under arrest for crimes against the Roman Empire."

The old man laid down his pen and took a deep breath. It was finished. He stood. Though old, the Great Hannibal Barca retained the confident posture of a legendary war general. He glanced toward the door, waiting for the pounding to start. He was surprised it had taken them this long to find him. In the years since his homeland was destroyed, he had worked for hire for Greece, Syria, and anyone that was against the Roman expansion. His children had married foreigners. His wife had died peacefully in her sleep some time ago. He was alone now. He was ready.

"Open up!" a Roman outside shouted.

Hannibal took a small pouch from his belt and poured

white powder into the goblet of wine on his desk. Then he shuffled to the latched double doors across the room from the pounding. His steps revealed his pride as much as his frailty. He summoned all of his strength, unlatched the doors and threw them open.

The piercing glare of afternoon sun splashed across the room and momentarily blinded him. But it didn't matter. He already knew what he would see: a fully armed company of soldiers waited for him below, as if they expected him to have a strategy that might require half a legion of soldiers to subdue him. He did have a strategy, so in a way, they were right to come prepared. But this was the kind of strategy all the legions in Rome couldn't stop.

Hannibal stepped out onto the balcony. The city square below him was packed with Roman soldiers and townspeople who had come to watch the spectacle.

A centurion stepped forward and looked up at Hannibal, tilting his head up and drawing his sword, as if defending himself against a ghost.

Hannibal smirked. "I expected you some time ago."

"Scipio Africanus has died," the centurion said, "and with him ends your protection from the Roman law."

The smirk fell from Hannibal's face. "I never asked him for protection."

"Does it please you to learn of your adversary's death?"

Hannibal was silent for a moment, not breaking eye contact with the centurion. "Scipio was the only Roman I ever respected. Now, only hatred remains."

The Roman centurion smiled. "Don't worry. We don't intend to kill you now. Rome awaits a parade with you in a cage."

Hannibal did his best to disguise his rage. After all, he was holding the drink in his hands that would wipe the indulgent smile off the centurion's face.

With a defiant stare, Hannibal lifted the goblet to his lips and tipped it back. It slid down his throat, warm and bitter.

"No!" the centurion shouted.

Shouts surrounded him as the townspeople watching realized what he had done.

Hannibal felt the life draining from his body. Seconds to eternity. The goblet fell from his hand, clanking on the balcony's tiles. He sank to his knees.

"Lion of Carthage," he said.

The door to the room finally slammed open behind him, and the room filled with soldiers.

"On the balcony!" a man yelled. He ran to Hannibal and knelt, pressing his hand to the old man's heart.

It was too late.

Hannibal Barca slumped to the side. The battle with Rome had ended.

Made in the USA
Las Vegas, NV
04 November 2020